PRAISE FOR:
Christmas Weddings Are The ~~Worst~~ Best

Marie Hobbs specializes in creating characters you love—and even a few you loathe. Compelling storytelling creates a safe space for romance and humor, infusing her later-in-life romances with authenticity. Realistic plotlines and relatable characters are woven through unexpected detours that leave you turning the pages into the wee hours. Cultural references prompt laugh-out-loud moments and an enthusiasm to read more about a community that feels like family and friends. Intriguing dialogue and well-paced plotlines do not disappoint. Marie Hobbs is the fresh voice we've been longing for.
—Lilka Raphael, author,
www.lilkaraphaelcom.wordpress.com

Author Marie Hobbs is a talented and discerning reader herself, so cheers on this rising romance star! Known for her knack for creating characters that charm and occasionally challenge, Hobbs infuses the scene with a blend of humor and heart. Her storytelling—a delightful mix of romance and wit set within engaging, believable worlds—keeps readers giggling and guessing late into the night. With rich cultural nods that spark joy and foster curiosity, her stories feel like catching up with old friends— familiar, warm, and full of surprises. Sharp dialogue and a brisk pace make her work a fresh voice in the genre, one I believe is destined to rise even higher.
—Janese Dixon, best-selling romance author,
www.danjatales.com

Christmas Weddings

Are The ~~Worst~~ Best

Marie Hobbs

Christmas Weddings are the ~~Worst~~ Best, Marie Hobbs
Issued in electronic and paperback formats
Paperback ISBN: 978-1-970354-01-0
E-book ISBN: 978-1-970354-02-7
First Edition

Publisher: Dressed in Love Press, LLC
www.drkatherinehayes.com

Cover Designer: Katherine Hutchinson-Hayes
Book Interior Designer: Jenifer Jennings

Printed in the United States of America

To everyone who's ever dreamed of love wrapped in grace and laughter—this story is for you. And to my readers who believe that even life's detours are part of God's design, may you always find joy in the journey and peace in His timing. Writing stories that honor faith, hope, and love has been one of my greatest blessings, and I pray that Christmas Weddings are the ~~Worst~~ Best brings a smile to your heart and a reminder that God's plan is always perfect—even when it doesn't go as planned.

Prologue: Alex

Nine months earlier…

"Hold it. Hold it. Perfect." *Click. Click.* "Now, a little to your left. Chin up a bit. Good." *Click. Click.*

Alex looked on while the photographer flipped through the digital images of Monique in the third outfit she'd brought for her Top 40 Professionals under 40 photoshoot.

He was leasing a townhouse near Monique and had bought the condo in Memphis as an investment property. They were together much more than they were apart, and not just because Atlanta was their primary residence. As a senior implementation manager, he had to return to the Memphis office at least once a quarter. Since Monique and Jessica were building their client list in Memphis, Monique had the flexibility to coordinate her visits with Alex's OBS meetings.

Jessica was right. Dual residence did look good on social media.

The photographer looked at his assistant and smiled, clearly pleased with his work.

"Okay, that's a wrap," his assistant announced to the room.

The photographer said a few words to Monique and hugged her.

"Well done," his assistant said to Monique as she walked over to Alex.

"How did I look?" she asked after she released him from a hug.

"Beautiful, as always."

He always told her that because it was always true.

"Even in my satin bonnet, ratty T-shirt, dolphin pajama pants, and fuzzy slippers?" She wore a teasing smile.

"Especially in your satin bonnet, ratty T-shirt, dolphin pajama pants, and fuzzy slippers."

She gave him her "yeah-right" look, but blushed at his compliment.

"Is there anything left in the dressing room? I've already loaded up your earlier outfits."

"Just those last two bags." She pointed to an overnight bag and a duffel bag next to the chair he'd been sitting in.

The coordinator of the Atlanta Business Alliance Top 40 program joined them.

"Good job, Monique. Do you have any questions?"

"No, Kacy, I can't think of any."

It was Alex's opportunity.

"I have a question."

Both women turned to face him.

Alex dropped to one knee, pulled a ring box out of his pocket, and opened it. Monique's hands flew to her cheeks, and her mouth formed an O. The room that had been bustling with activity went completely silent.

"Monique Lovelace, will you marry me?"

There was a time in his life when Alex never thought he'd ever get the chance to say those words. He was ecstatic to be wrong. Then he heard the words that he would remember for the rest of his life.

"Yes, Alexander Patterson, I absolutely will!"

He slid the ring on her finger and stood to kiss her. But before he could, she launched herself into his arms. The room erupted in cheers, whistles, and claps.

To people who didn't know them, their getting engaged after only four months of dating probably seemed too fast. But in his mind, the proposal was twenty-three years late.

Monique released him, then slapped her forehead with her palm.

"We'd better get going. I have the Raineshaven BBQ Let Me Reintroduce Myself Grand Re-opening in Memphis tomorrow. Is the luggage already in the truck?"

"Yes, ma'am. Time to hit the road." They rushed out to the parking deck.

After they were buckled up, Alex started their truck and pulled out onto Peachtree Street.

"So, Monie Love, what do you think about a Christmas Wedding?"

Chapter 1: Alex
Here Come the Bride and Groom

Thursday, December 5 — 16 days until the wedding

Alex Patterson parked in one of the designated spaces for his Memphis condo. A few of his neighbors' doors were already decked out with wreaths, lights, and bells. Maybe he'd decorate this year. He had an extra dose of Christmas spirit, for good reason. He glanced at the console screen.

Two o'clock. Right on schedule.

The drive from Atlanta had been uneventful. A stark contrast from his trip along the same route in December of the year before. He smiled at the memory.

But it ended well. The best it could have, actually. Thank You, God.

His text message chime drew his eyes to the message preview, ending his reminiscing. It was Lisa, a high school classmate and a colleague at Owens Business Services.

"Probably about the OBS holiday party."

His thoughts immediately went to the prior year's party—his and Monique's first official date, causing his smile to grow wider.

A minute later, Monique Lovelace pulled into the space next to him. Typically, they rode together, but since they had divided some of the final tasks, each needed their own transportation.

He dropped his phone in his jacket pocket and reached for the door handle. "I'll read Lisa's text later. There are more important things to tend to right now."

He stepped out to greet his beautiful fiancée with a hug and a kiss. It had been over three hours since their stop at the travel center, and he had missed her. Monique stepped out of her sporty SUV and into Alex's waiting arms.

"Alexander Patterson."

Her voice was muffled as she spoke into his shoulder, but that didn't diminish the warm feeling of hearing her special name for him. He lifted her chin with his finger, bringing them face to face.

"Monie Love." He responded with his special name for her.

She rose onto her toes and kissed him on the cheek. He was tempted to forget their post-arrival plans and dive into the fun stuff, but the day would've gotten chaotic if they strayed from the schedule. They had carefully planned every detail so that the pre-ceremony activities and the wedding would run smoothly. So, he reluctantly shifted into project manager mode.

Alex released her and stepped back. "You go inside. I'll unload my luggage, and then we can debrief."

"Okay. I'll bring in the snacks and drinks. What's left of them."

"Sounds like a plan." He couldn't resist kissing her on the forehead.

Alex grabbed a suitcase and a garment bag from the back seat of his extended-cab pickup truck and reflected on his earlier conversation with his parents. It had confirmed his decision to stay at his condo rather than with them. They were very excited about the wedding and wanted to talk about it. All. The. Time.

Not that he wasn't excited. Marrying Monique was truly a dream come true. But was it wrong to want to talk about other topics, like they used to before he and Monique got engaged? Did getting married mean the other parts of his life would disappear? Or that he should ignore everyone else?

Of course not.

Alex wondered whether his internal response was the "right" one. Was he supposed to give up everything else to focus on his marriage? He'd done that with Brionne. But just because it didn't save his former marriage didn't necessarily mean it wasn't the right thing to do.

Or did it?

Alex shook off his questioning and reviewed all of the supporting evidence for his choice of lodging.

The condo would be a refuge when he or Monique needed a break from their loving, well-meaning families.

It provided a cozy, private space without adding another line item to the budget for their dinner party with the bridesmaids and groomsmen.

Marquis was a few doors down, so Alex could easily make sure he was keeping up with his best man duties.

And no one applied to rent it over the Christmas holidays, so it would have sat empty otherwise.

Alex brought in his last bag and found Monique sitting at the table in the dining nook, tapping away on her laptop. No doubt going over one of their wedding spreadsheets. He grabbed his backpack and joined her.

While his laptop booted up, he took a bag of potato chips from the table. "Should we review by category or day?"

Monique extended a mini-pack of baby carrots to him.

"If you didn't want me to eat the chips, why did you buy them and then put them on the table?"

"Did I say don't eat the chips? I'm just offering you something healthy to go with them." She punctuated her comment with a sweet smile.

He sighed, put down the chips, and took the carrots. "Fine. But I'm eating the chips, too."

"Uh-huh. And to answer your question, let's go over the schedule by day."

Of course, their calendars were entirely in sync. It's what they did.

Alex was ready for a break after sending meeting reminders to their family, wedding party, vendors, and wedding coordinator. He opened a food delivery app and turned his screen to face Monique.

"I thought we'd have a quiet dinner together before you go to your brother's house until the wedding."

Monique gathered her twists into a low bun with what Alex had learned was a scrunchie.

"Sounds good. But I plan for us to have dinner together every day. Except for the bachelor and bachelorette parties." She leaned back in the chair and exhaled. "Everything is done." She counted them off on her fingers while she spoke. "We have the marriage license. All the vendors are confirmed. Our final fittings are scheduled. We finished our pre-marital counseling three weeks ago, and our meetings with our former pastors are all set for tomorrow."

Alex stood and stretched while Monique scrolled through their dinner options. "True. Why do people say weddings are chaotic?"

She shook her head and looked up at him. "Poor planning."

He thought back to the wedding with Brione. She was running around and almost hysterical at times. He hadn't been involved because Brionne and her mother did everything. His only responsibilities had been to order the tux they picked out and show up at the places and times they put on his calendar.

Monique was a public relations professional. He was a senior implementation manager and a certified Project Management Professional. They planned for a living. The days leading up to their wedding would feel like a vacation.

"You're right. And since we don't have that problem, these two weeks will be smooth sailing."

***

After dinner, Alex and Monique cuddled on the couch to watch her favorite Christmas movie, *Jingle Jangle*, and his, *Die Hard*. Monique had given up trying to convince him that *Die Hard* wasn't a Christmas movie. He smiled to himself. Good thing, because he wasn't budging on that.

He faced the TV, but his mind was on what would happen on December 21st. He'd marry Monique. While technically it was his second marriage, it felt as if it were his first. After all, Monique was his first love. The feelings of eagerness and anticipation for the wedding were new to him.

He drew circles on Monique's shoulder. She turned to face him.

"It's happening. Isn't it?"

She smiled and nodded. "It is. You nervous?"

He wasn't nervous in a bad way. His restlessness was more about waiting for the fulfillment of his deepest desire.

He shook his head. "No. You?"

"Not at all."

She sounded calm and confident, but then she bit her bottom lip and quickly shifted her gaze from him to him again, so fast he almost missed it.

"You ready?" she asked.

Her question carried a hint of insecurity, so he closed the little space between them.

"Yes. Ready for us to be husband and wife…for many reasons." He was certain his expression telegraphed one reason in particular.

"Alex…"

She placed her hand on his chest and gently pushed. He didn't move. Instead, he dislodged the twist at her right temple from her bun and twirled it around his finger. After nearly a year together, she still shivered when he played with her hair. He loved that.

"Since we're going to have some free time, maybe we can catch some of the MMC activities."

Being forced to work together on the Merry Memphis Christmas Festival, or MMC as they later called it, the year before, reunited them as friends and gave them the chance to grow closer. With a bit of unsolicited help from their families.

Monique's expression brightened. "That would be fun. Any particular ones you have in mind?"

"Anywhere there's mistletoe."

"Alex…"

He lifted his hand and shrugged. "What? Can't a man…"

His question was interrupted by their text chimes. They reached for their phones.

"It's from the pastors," they said in unison.

Pastor Mike: Alex and Monique, we're sorry for the late notice. As you know, this is a hectic time for our churches. Instead of meeting me at my office tomorrow morning, Pastor Reginald, Pastor Cynthia, and I will do a virtual call with you. It's at the same time, so just click the link below, and we'll go from there. Good night.

Alex's stomach dropped.

"Huh."

Was Monique's one-syllable response as loaded as his thoughts? He immediately talked himself down.

The meetings with their Memphis pastors mainly were a formality. They had already completed an eight-week premarital counseling course at their church in Atlanta. However, out of respect for the influence their childhood pastors and Alex's most recent Memphis pastor had on their lives, they wanted to give each of them a chance to talk with the couple before the wedding. This was especially important since they had asked them to officiate.

"It's not a big deal. This won't throw anything off. In fact, by talking to them all at once, we free up two hours plus travel time."

Monique nodded. "Exactly. I'll come here in the morning, and we'll dial in. Everything is still on track."

"Yeah. This is good."

***

Friday, December 6 — 15 days until the wedding

Friday morning, Alex's doorbell rang, a key turned in the lock, and the deadbolt released with a thud.

"Good morning, soon-to-be hubby. I brought breakfast. But the coffee is in the car. I couldn't carry it all."

He had his jacket and shoes on before Monique finished her last sentence. "Your mom's hazelnut Arabica bean coffee?"

"Yeah, she and Dad came over to see me once I got to RJ's and ended up staying over." She tilted her head. "Now that I think about it, they must have planned to, since her coffee was there."

He met her in the front room, took the bag of breakfast sandwiches, and kissed her. Her eyes brightened with pleasure.

"Keep that up, and the coffee will get cold."

He tightened his embrace. "As much as I love that coffee, it's no comparison to you."

However, they had a meeting to attend, so he released her, put the food on the sofa table, and retrieved the coffee from her SUV. After he returned, Alex blessed the food, and they ate.

Ten minutes before they were to log in, their conversation was interrupted by a phone call. Alex checked his phone. It was Lisa.

Two days in a row.

"Let me take this. It might be about work."

"Hey, Lisa. What's up?"

"Hey, Alex. I'm just checking on you. Making sure you arrived safely."

"Yeah, we got in yesterday afternoon. I saw your text, but we had," he looked at Monique and winked, "some things to do."

Monique blushed.

"Oh, yeah, of course. Um, I know you're on vacation, but are you stopping by the office while you're here?"

Monique gathered the trash and took it to the kitchen.

"Am I needed for anything specific?" He'd made sure to either close out or delegate any open issues before he left Atlanta.

"No, no, nothing like that. Just asking."

"Well, if there's time, I might drop in. Other than that, we'll see you all at the wedding."

"Oh, okay." Lisa sounded disappointed.

"I hate to cut this short, but we have a call in a few minutes. So, I'll catch up with you later."

"Yes. Go, go. I'll talk to you later.

Alex disconnected the call just as Monique returned.

"What was that about?"

"It was Lisa. I think they may be planning a surprise for us. She asked whether I plan to go into the office while I'm here."

"That's nice."

"Yeah, it is." He glanced at his watch. "We'd better log on."

He opened the site and clicked the Join the Meeting button. Within seconds, all three pastors were online.

"Well, good morning. Promptness is a good sign." Pastor Mike, Alex's childhood pastor, greeted them.

Alex and Monique responded in kind.

"We all have busy schedules, so let's get right to it," Pastor Cynthia, Monique's childhood co-pastor, said.

"Each of us has a special history with and love for you, Monique and Alex. And we would be remiss to conduct your wedding ceremony without a deeper understanding of you as a couple."

Alex was suddenly queasy. He snuck a side glance at Monique. She sat stiffly, straining to smile.

Why do I have the feeling I'm not going to like what I'm about to hear?

Pastor Reginald, the pastor of the church Alex joined when he returned to Memphis, took over. "We've agreed upon ten topics that we need to ensure you understand," he paused, "*before* we can officiate and Pastor Cynthia can sign the marriage license with a clear conscience."

Ten topics? We have a meeting with our coordinator in an hour and a half!

"So," Pastor Reginald continued, "over the next week and a half, you'll have three pre-marital counseling sessions with each of us individually, then a final meeting with all of us together."

Pastor Reginald smiled as if he hadn't made a completely outrageous request—no, requirement— that would throw their lives into absolute disarray.

Pastor Mike spoke. "Normally, we would have at least two days, most times a week, between sessions so that you can discuss any issues that come up. But we don't have time for that. This will have to be an accelerated program, and you'll need to fit in your conversations in the evenings."

Alex and Monique turned to face each other. He was sure the look of shock on Monique's face matched his. He cleared his throat.

Think of this as a demanding client who wants a nine-week implementation completed in a month.

He placed his hand on his chest. "First, thank you, Pastors, for investing in us and our future as a couple. We," he took Monique's hand in his, "went through an eight-week pre-marital course at our church in Atlanta. It was quite thorough. We can provide the curriculum and our certificate of completion. Hopefully, that will address any concerns you have."

Pastor Cynthia offered an indulgent smile. "Yes, I know your current pastor and the program at your church. And I agree—it's great. However, you asked us to officiate. And we don't do so unless we've spent time personally with you as a couple."

He squeezed Monique's hand, hoping her public relations skills could persuade them to change their minds. She took the hint.

"Of course, Pastor Cynthia. That's why we set up an individual meeting with each of you." Monique reached for her laptop. "If you could just review the curriculum, I'm sure you'd all find that it's–"

Pastor Mike's brow was furrowed when he leaned into the camera. "Are you against additional counseling?"

They both responded. "No! Of course not!"

It was going downhill. There had to be a way to rein it in.

"Additional meetings aren't on our calendar. calendar," Alex clarified.

"We have meetings with our wedding planner, vendors, families, and wedding party almost every day leading up to the wedding," Monique added.

"We've scheduled these two weeks to the minute." Alex shifted in his seat. "It'll be hard to add ten more meetings and the resulting homework."

"I know this is a surprise, but we all believe it's necessary," Pastor Mike explained. "That's why we've adjusted our schedules to make time for it. Since these sessions will benefit you, we thought you two would be even more willing to do so."

"But we planned—"

"Are you planning for a marriage or just a wedding?" Pastor Cynthia asked.

"Why are you getting married?" Pastor Mike quickly followed.

"Why each other and not someone else?" Pastor Reginald added.

Alex and Monique turned wide eyes to each other again. They weren't going to win this one.

"By the way," Pastor Reginald said, "neither of those questions counts as a session."

Alex still hadn't found his voice, nor had his future wife, but Pastor Mike kept the meeting going.

"I just emailed you the schedule based on our availability. The first one is with me tomorrow. We don't usually schedule Saturday sessions, but again, we realize that time is of the essence."

Monique turned her laptop toward Alex, displaying the counseling schedule and their schedule side by side.

"Review it and let us know as soon as possible if any sessions need to be rescheduled. All ten need to be completed by December 19th."

They all said goodbye and signed off.

Monique looked shell-shocked. "What just happened?"

Alex exhaled slowly and waved his hands.

"Okay, our perfect plan has suffered a blow, but it's not demolished. It's normal to have to make some last-minute adjustments. Right?"

Monique's eyes were fixed on her laptop screen. "True. Today, we need to give the initial guest count to the caterer, print the place cards, and start creating the seating plan. I have my final fitting and need to break in my shoes." She looked up at him. "You need to make an appointment for a haircut and break in your shoes, too."

"Break in my shoes? I don't think so."

She shrugged. "Okay. No complaining about your feet hurting during the receiving line."

I probably should break in my shoes.

She turned back to her laptop. "But surprisingly, we're free for all the sessions as scheduled. Maybe…maybe God is reminding us to keep our marriage in focus amid all of the wedding tasks."

"Yeah, I can see that. It's easy to concentrate on the details and lose sight of the overall vision."

Even though they agreed that they could easily accommodate the unexpected change in plans, an uneasiness was lodged in his chest. Monique's eyes indicated the same was true for her. He sighed.

Hopefully—prayerfully—there wouldn't be any other surprises.

Chapter 2: Monique
Something Old

Saturday, December 7 — 14 days until the wedding

Monique quietly reflected on the previous day's events that had brought them to that moment. She was on her way to the first of three pre-marital counseling sessions with Pastor Mike. Talk about a bombshell.

They couldn't have given us a heads-up instead of catching us completely off guard?

Maybe that was the point. They wanted to see how she and Alex would react to an unforeseen change of plans. Still, she would have preferred that they had picked a different way. Thankfully, the meeting with the wedding planner went smoothly without any surprises.

"Monie, you good?"

She turned to face him. "Yeah. Why?"

"You're awfully quiet over there?"

"Are you trying to say I talk a lot?"

Alex smirked. "I was going to say that you usually prefer conversation to silence, but if the tongue fits…"

She shook her head. "If you weren't driving my truck right now…"

The true owner of the pickup truck was the subject of ongoing debate. Alex subconsciously bought

Monique's dream truck down to the smallest detail, but he didn't realize it until they reconnected the year before.

"Your truck? My name is on the registration. So, legally, it's mine."

"Well, starting December 21st, legally, it'll be mine, too."

He raised his eyebrow in defiance.

"Yep, right after you say, 'with all my worldly goods I thee endow.'"

"I'm going to have to talk to Pastor Cynthia about taking that part out of the ceremony." He pretended to mumble under his breath.

"Good luck with that."

The familiar sight of Metropolitan Christian Church came into view. Alex parked and unbuckled his seatbelt. "You ready?"

He extended his palm to her. She put her hand in his.

"Always and forever until the end of time."

***

Monique stood next to Alex as he rapped on Pastor Mike's office doorframe. Pastor Mike looked up from whatever he was working on and set it aside. His office was warm and inviting, like the man himself, and adorned with modest Christmas decorations.

A Nativity scene carved from wood sat on top of the bookcase behind his desk. A small tree decorated with multicolored ball ornaments and white twinkle lights stood in the far corner of the room, and a potted poinsettia rested on the small round side table.

"Monique. Alex." Pastor Mike stood and extended his arms. "Please come in." He motioned to a small couch against the far wall. He closed his office door and then sat in one of the two leather wingback chairs across from the couch.

"Normally, my wife would join me, but she's at the play rehearsal. She'll join us for the next two. Let's open with prayer."

After praying for Monique and Alex as individuals and as a couple, Pastor Mike asked for God's guidance for the session and for any hidden issues that could affect their union to be revealed.

Monique's stomach clenched. Did the small niggling of doubt that occasionally surfaced count as a hidden thing? No, of course not. Every article she read said it was normal. Maybe Alex was hiding something.

Before Monique could recall whether Alex had been acting suspiciously, Pastor Mike said "amen" and started the session.

"Each session covers a topic mentioned in wedding phrases or vows. Today's session is Something Old."

"Oh, like something old, something blue, something borrowed, something blue." Monique smiled.

"Exactly." Pastor Mike steepled his fingers together. "Do you know the meaning behind that poem?"

Monique tilted her head, then looked at Alex. He shook his head.

"No, I don't. I never thought about it." She felt her cheeks warm.

Should I have?

"It's okay," Pastor Mike assured them. "I didn't know either when I got married. In fact, I had officiated at least a hundred weddings before I did. Many times, we do things out of tradition, but we don't consider whether they're good, necessary, or beneficial."

Alex nodded. "True. So, what does it mean?"

"Traditionally, the item represents the connection between the bride's past and her family, acting as a link to her ancestors and heritage. However, a marriage brings together two families' heritages and traditions. Sometimes, these can clash."

Pastor Mike put on his glasses and opened his notebook. "So, we're going to talk about family traditions and how they'll play a part in your marriage. Christmas is a good time to start thinking about this since it's a season full of traditions."

"Oh, that shouldn't be a problem. Our families have known each other for twenty-eight years." Alex spoke with confidence.

"They have wanted us to be together for years," Monique agreed. "And they love each other, and us. Sometimes, even taking the side of the non-blood child." She cut her eyes at Alex.

He squeezed her hand. "Just because your mother makes her special hazelnut coffee for me doesn't mean she loves you any less. She just loves me more." He grinned at her.

Monique rolled her eyes and then looked at Pastor Mike. "You were his childhood pastor. Couldn't you have fixed this?"

"Some things, Monique, only God can do. But back to the topic. Have you spent Christmas with each other's families?"

Monique opened her mouth to confirm, then stopped. She looked at Alex, then back at Pastor Mike.

"Well, no. Not really. We worked in the Christmas Store when we were kids. And we went caroling. But as kids and in college, all the major Christmas activities were spent with our respective families."

Alex nodded. "Last year, we met up at some of the MMC activities. And we decorated the tree with each family, but mostly, our family Christmas traditions were done apart."

Monique realized in that moment that she and Alex had never really spent a Christmas together. The look on Alex's face said it hadn't occurred to him either.

"Okay then," Pastor Mike said, "here's the first activity for this session."

First?

He handed each of them a steno pad and a pen.

Analog. Gotta love Pastor Mike for being old school. But there is something to be said for writing things down versus typing them.

"I want you to write down two Christmas traditions that are important to you." He wagged his finger at them. "And no peeking at each other's paper."

Monique started writing immediately.

This is an easy one.

"Pens down," Pastor Mike ordered after five minutes.

Monique had finished in three. She had no doubt what her must-haves were.

"Monique, why don't you share one of yours?"

"Okay. My family always attends our church's rendition of Handel's *Messiah* on the third Sunday in December." She turned to Alex, expecting to see him smiling as much as she was at the memory.

He was not.

"Alex," Pastor Mike spoke gently, "how do you feel about that?"

"Well," he turned his scrunched-up face from Monique to Pastor Mike and pointed to his notepad, "my family decorates our tree and house on the third Sunday. We laugh, talk, and have dinner. It's more interactive than sitting down and listening to singing."

Monique's right eyebrow involuntarily arched up. "Are you suggesting that your activity is more important than mine?"

"I mean… You said that before last year, you were only in town from Christmas Eve until about the twenty-seventh. How is it a holiday tradition if you haven't been in years?" He turned to Pastor Mike. "Right?"

She didn't wait for Pastor Mike to give his opinion.

"I grew up going every year, and I love it. And Mr. Know-It-All, I stream it when I'm in Atlanta. But when I'm here, I go in person."

"You didn't go last year."

"That's because you invited me to decorate with you and your family, and then we had dinner. By the time we finished, the *Messiah* had already started."

"Well, see," he lifted his hands and shrugged, "it's not a hardcore tradition. You skipped it last year, so it shouldn't be a big deal to skip it again."

Monique turned in her seat to face Alex fully. When she opened her mouth to share her thoughts on Alex's comments, Pastor Mike spoke.

"Alex, you can't decide for Monique how important something is to her. Further discussion on this topic will be your homework."

They nodded their agreement.

"Alex, share a tradition you wrote down."

He cleared his throat. "On Christmas Eve, everyone opens one family gift."

What?

"You open presents on Christmas Eve? That's practically a crime."

"You and I exchanged presents on Christmas Eve in high school."

"Yeah, because we spend the whole day with our families on Christmas. You can exchange gifts with others before Christmas, but the presents under the tree are only opened on Christmas Day. Most years, we didn't even wrap them until Christmas Eve."

She turned to Pastor Mike since he was the only other reasonable person in the room.

"Every Christmas morning, we gather in the sitting

room and have a devotion. We sing carols, read the passage about Jesus' birth aloud, and then pray. After that, we open presents. It's a reminder for the kids—for all of us, really—of the true meaning of the day."

"Are you implying that my family doesn't know the true meaning of Christmas because we open a present on Christmas Eve?" Alex's voice pitched up an octave.

She shook her head. "I didn't say—"

"Okay," Pastor Mike interrupted. "I think we've identified another homework assignment." He clasped his hands and rested them on his lap. "There's one more part of the past we need to look into."

There's more?

Monique still felt some kind of way about the first activity.

"You need to know and trust your fiancé's past."

Alex spoke first. "We've talked about my previous marriage and her previous engagement."

Pastor Mike nodded. "That's important, and it's good that you have shared that with each other. But you also have to trust your fiancé's past with you."

"What do you mean?" They asked in unison.

Regardless of what some people might try to tell you, every marriage has its highs and lows. To move forward after a 'down', you need to trust each other to learn from it and do better next time.

He gestured to their notepads. "Now, I want each of you to write down two memories from your relationship—one positive and one negative. Then write down what you learned from each one."

After five minutes, Pastor Mike asked Monique to share one of her memories.

Monique glanced down at her paper, over to Alex, then at Pastor Mike.

"Before last year, Alex and I hadn't spoken in ten years. He ghosted me." She felt Alex stiffen in the chair beside her. "Obviously, we talked about it, but I learned that we must continue to communicate and be honest with each other, even when the truth is difficult and unpleasant. It's the only way for us to stay connected."

Pastor Mike nodded.

"I thought we'd moved past that," Alex said without looking at her.

She faced him. "Yes, I've forgiven you and no longer hold it against you, but I shouldn't discard what I learned from it.

He met her eyes. "It feels like you're throwing it in my face."

"How am I throwing it in your face if I'm using it as an example of how we've grown as a couple?"

At least, I thought we'd grown as a couple.

"You know I don't like to think about that." He threw up his hands. "You couldn't have picked another example? Why was that the first thing that came to your mind?"

"Because *this* challenging moment hadn't happened yet."

"Okay, okay. Breathe," Pastor Mike calmly told them. "Alex, you obviously don't like talking about the years you didn't communicate. But how do you feel about what Monique said she learned?"

"It's fine," Alex replied, again without looking at her.

It was clear to Monique, and she was sure Pastor Mike too, that Alex was not at all "fine."

The first few bars of *God Rest Ye Merry Gentlemen* sounded, and Pastor Mike turned the alarm off.

"We've reached the end of our session."

Thank God.

Your homework, Monique and Alex, is to discuss your conflicting traditions. Listen to each other without judging. You don't need to solve everything today, but you should develop a general approach.

Monique exhaled and shifted in her seat. Alex dropped his gaze to the floor.

"Now, let's join hands and pray for God to guide you in blending your pasts into a future filled with love, faith, and joy."

***

Monique and Alex got in the truck and headed to the Christmas Store for the first family meeting. They chose the Christmas Store because they reconnected there a year prior. But as they rode in uncomfortable silence and Monique still fumed over some of Alex's comments, the idea wasn't as cute or perfect as it had been weeks ago.

Monique squirmed, wishing she were driving

herself alone—to give her much-needed space from Alex. But her car was at her brother's house and retrieving it meant talking to Alex. She didn't want to talk to him. Listening to him during the counseling session had been bad enough, and he had no desire for more unpleasantness.

Even though she was facing the window, Monique sensed him periodically glance at her. Out of the corner of her eye, she noticed his grip tighten on the steering wheel and the muscle in his jaw tighten as he clenched his teeth.

Good. He's as irritated as I am.

When they arrived at the Christmas Store, several familiar cars were in the parking lot, even though the meeting wasn't scheduled to start for another ten minutes. She and Alex silently got out of the car.

Monique entered and looked for her family. Her mother and father were shelving toys. RJ, her brother, and Yvette, his wife, were stocking the registers. Her Auntie Thelma appeared to be supervising their work. She turned right to join the other Lovelaces without saying a word to Alex. However, she glanced over her shoulder to see that Alex had gone left to join his mother, father, and Auntie Anne, who were hanging clothes on the racks.

"You know, Anne and I are supposed to only be advising this year. You and Alex are supposed to be running the Merry Memphis Christmas Festival." Auntie Thelma wagged her finger at Monique, but her twinkling eyes and wide smile revealed she wasn't really upset.

Monique tilted her head, then hugged her aunt. "You love it, and you know you do."

Her mother opened her arms wide. "Hi, Honey."

Monique reveled in her mother's embrace. Then her mother released her, stepped back, and studied her face. "How was your session?"

Monique glanced over her shoulder at Alex's back, then turned back to her mother. "We have homework." She tried to keep the irritation out of her voice. "Seriously. Homework. We're supposed to—"

"Sis!"

Monique spun around at Stacey's greeting and hurried over to meet her. Tara, the other member of The Crew who lived in Memphis, entered, followed by Alex's best friend, Marquis.

"What's going on?" Tara asked as she looked Monique over. "You look irritated."

Stacey nodded in agreement.

Monique exhaled sharply. "We had an argument during our session this morning with Pastor Mike. What does that say about us?" She glanced across the room and saw Alex talking privately with Marquis, then nodded toward them. "He's probably complaining to Marq right now."

"Please, you should have seen Nick and me," Tara said with a flick of her wrist. "Counseling sessions are designed to poke the sore spots. Every couple has to work through this. We did. The two of you can, too."

Can we?

Monique suppressed the nagging feeling when Elise, the wedding coordinator, approached with Alex in tow.

"Are we ready?"

Monique locked eyes with Alex, then quickly averted her gaze. They nodded.

"Great."

Monique stood on one side of Elise and Alex on the other as she got everyone's attention.

"Good afternoon. If everyone can take a seat, we can get started."

Everyone settled into the chairs arranged into two rows.

"Thank you for being here," Elise gestured to those seated, "whether in person," she nodded to Tina, Kendra, Aniya, and Desiree on the large flat screen monitor, "or virtually. And an extra thank you from Ms. Anne and Ms. Thelma to all those who came early to help set up the Christmas Store."

After light applause, Elise continued.

"I'm Elise Daniels, the wedding coordinator, and I'm honored that Monique and Alex chose me to bring their special day to life. Let's open with prayer." She turned to her left. "Alex?" When he didn't answer, she turned to her right. "Monique?"

Monique didn't respond either, but she did see her parents and Alex's parents exchange a look.

Elise clasped her hands together. "Okay, I'll be glad to do the honors."

While Elsie prayed, Monique reflected on the counseling session. Her reaction was unusual. Obstacles often appeared in her business. Troubleshooting and finding common ground were among her strengths. And it wasn't as if it was the first time she and Alex had disagreed. So, why was she so upset? Why was she questioning her decision?

Is this what people mean by pre-wedding jitters?

A chorus of amens halted Monique's thoughts.

Elise walked through the pared-down schedule, which included only those activities involving the wedding party. Somewhere between final fittings and the bachelor and bachelorette parties, Monique's mind wandered again.

Had it really been only a year since she was shelving toys like her parents had done earlier? Some days, it felt like a decade had passed. Other days, it was just the week before. She warmed at the memories of reconnecting with the old Alex and discovering the new Alex. A slight smile touched her lips.

Monique tuned back in as Elise finished giving her instructions about the ceremony. Luckily, she knew all the details, so she hadn't missed anything during her walk down memory lane.

"Any questions?"

Thomas, Alex's dad, raised his hand, then stood.

"I know the 'something old' is usually given to the bride…"

Monique's stomach dropped at his words. She felt Alex's eyes on her. Had he told his father about their argument? She tried not to look over at Alex, but she couldn't resist his pull. His face echoed her surprise. He shook his head slightly.

"…but," Thomas pulled a velvet jewelry box from his pocket, "every Patterson man since my great, great grandfather, the talented silversmith who handmade these cuff links, has worn them at his wedding. And I," he cleared his throat, "I would be honored, Alex, if you did the same."

Is this the first time he's wearing them? Or is this yet another wedding thing he's done before?

Alex blinked his eyes rapidly as Thomas handed him the box. After he opened it, his face contorted in confusion.

"It's empty, Dad."

"What?" Thomas' eyes widened. "They were in there when I got here." He scanned the floor frantically. "They… they must have fallen out."

Monique's father stood. "Okay. Let's not panic. They must be here. Thomas, what areas did you work in today?"

"I was almost everywhere. Remember, Richard? We were in the storeroom, then by the registers, shelves, and clothing racks. Even in the office for a while."

"Let's split up," Richard suggested. "Everybody, grab a partner. Two sets of eyes are better than one."

"Right," Thomas agreed. "We'll split the areas in here. Monique and Alex, take the storage room."

"Keep away from the tinsel," Auntie Anne warned.

Monique flushed at Auntie Anne's mention of the almost-kiss moment she and Alex shared in the storeroom after a tinsel fight. Her mouth fell open when she realized it had happened a year prior to the day.

That's not happening today.

"One time, Auntie," Alex responded.

"Once is all it takes."

Monique heated even more at the veiled implication.

She and Alex went to the storeroom and started looking separately at opposite ends of the room. She checked the floor, shelves, and open boxes. Nothing. Eventually, they met in the middle of the room and stood face-to-face.

Monique opened her mouth to speak, but the door slammed against its frame and made her jump, trapping her words in her throat.

Alex met her eyes. "Something must have created a wind tunnel."

He turned the handle, but the door didn't budge. He grabbed the handle again and drove his shoulder into the door, throwing his weight behind it. The resultant grunt and thud echoed through the storage room, but the door remained in place. He knocked and called out. No one responded.

He walked back over to her and sighed. "It's stuck. Should we try to call someone?"

Monique raised her empty hands. "I didn't bring my purse, so I don't have my phone. Do you have yours?"

He patted his pockets. "I put it down when Dad handed me the box. I must have left it on the table."

"Guess we just have to wait."

"I guess so." He looked down at the floor, then back up at Monique.

"Look, Monie." "Hey, Alex." They spoke at the same time.

Nervous laughter came from both of them. Then Alex took Monique's hand.

"Look, Monie. This tradition thing isn't a showstopper. Our siblings figured it out. Certainly, they're not smarter than we are."

"Excellent point. I mean, if RJ figured it out, surely, we can too." She shook her head. "Taking a jab at RJ isn't as fun when he's not in the room."

He chuckled. "You'll have to make sure you say it in front of him later."

Monique laced her fingers with Alex's. "We're entering a new phase in life. Things have to change. We can take a little of yours, a little of mine, and something new to create our own traditions."

At least they were both from Memphis and could spend time with both families when they came. RJ and Tina's spouses were from different cities and had to alternate where they spent Christmas. So did Alex's sister, Kendra.

Alex took her other hand. "And the years when everyone comes to Memphis, we can do a big gathering for both sides. We could even host in Atlanta every once in a while."

Monique nodded. "It won't be the first adjustment for either of our families. I'm still not used to the family home being RJ and Yvette's place and my parents being in a condo."

"My parents adjusted to my joining a different church from them when I moved back. It took some conversations, but they realized it was best."

"And," Monique stepped closer to Alex, "we could exchange gifts privately with each other on Christmas Eve."

"I like your thinking, Monie Love." He pulled her to him. "And if the celebrating happens to continue into Christmas morning…" He kissed her neck right below her ear.

She shivered. "Alex…"

"I was insensitive about *The Messiah* and overly sensitive about your mentioning the rift. I'm sure we can finish decorating the tree and have dinner in time to make it to the musical."

"Technically, it is an oratorio," Monique started. At Alex's look, she changed course. "But that's not important. Continue."

He shook his head. "I know you didn't bring up the rift to punish or shame me. You were sharing how we grew from it." He sighed and rested his forehead against hers. "Whether I like it or not, the rift happened. I'm not proud of it, but pretending it didn't isn't real or healthy. I guess I'm still a bit embarrassed about how I acted, and I didn't want Pastor Mike to know. But that's something I have to work through."

"I'd never do anything to embarrass you, Alex." She paused. "Well, unless there's money involved."

They laughed, then wrapped their arms around each other and held tight.

I love this man.

She had to ask, or she'd be wondering all night.

"Alex," she said into his shoulder, "about the cufflinks—"

The door creaked open, stopping her mid-sentence.

"Found 'em!" Thomas happily proclaimed.

Alex released her from his embrace but kept his arm around her shoulders as they joined the others. To Monique's surprise, everyone sat at a table, talking, laughing, and snacking. They didn't look like they'd been searching at all.

"Mr. Patterson, where did you find them?"

"Monique, we're family. You can call me Dad Thomas." He pulled the cufflinks out of his pocket and extended them to Alex. "They were in my pocket the whole time. Must have fallen out of the box." He shrugged. "How about that?"

How about that, indeed.

Monique didn't ask how the cufflinks fell out of a closed box. She was just glad that she and Alex had made it through the first day of their second pre-marital counseling course intact.

Only nine more to go.

Chapter 3: Alex
Something New

Monday, December 9 – 12 days until the wedding

Monday morning, Alex was awoken by the ring of a video call.

"We're supposed to be sleeping in today," he grumbled.

Sunday had been a busy day. He and Monique spent time separately with both sets of parents, Auntie Anne, and Auntie Thelma before returning to the condo to review their week's schedule and handle Christmas cards. Afterwards, they watched movies, talked past midnight, and fell asleep on his couch. After making sure Monique got to her brother's house safely, Alex went to bed around 2:00 AM.

So, why was there a call at 8:00 AM from Elise? An unexpected call from the wedding coordinator usually meant bad news. But he decided to think positively, then tapped to join the call. His screen was filled with two faces, but only one of them brought a smile to his face.

"Hey, sweetheart," he said to Monique. "Hi, Elise. Did I miss a meeting?"

"No, but there is something I need to talk with the two of you about. Why don't we meet over breakfast today at Dee's Kitchen? My treat."

Elise's forced smile and overly cheerful tone made his heart beat faster.

"Should I ask why?"

Elise shook her head. "We'll talk about it over some great food. See you in thirty minutes."

***

Alex ordered last and handed his menu to the server, who retreated to the kitchen. He rested his arm on the back of the booth behind Monique and looked across the table at Elise.

"Ok, Elise. Give it to us straight."

Elise placed her clasped hands on the table and sighed.

"Your florist had a family emergency that required her to leave town. She's unsure whether she'll be able to return in time for the wedding."

He felt Monique tense up. So, he moved his arm from the booth to her shoulders, then gave her what he hoped was a reassuring squeeze.

"She reached out to a friend whose work she recommends, Blooms by Bethany," Elise continued, "but she didn't hear back from Bethany before she left. However, I have Bethany's contact information and will continue to try to reach her."

Monique wordlessly nodded.

Meanwhile, I've found three florists in the area who don't currently have events on the 21st and have scheduled meetings with them today. You'll be able to enjoy a leisurely lunch and relax before your next pre-marital counseling session.

Alex had an idea that might remedy the problem and ease his wife-to-be's concerns.

"Do we really need flowers? If it's going to be this much stress, why not just go without them?"

Monique and Elise looked at him like he had three heads and five arms.

Okay, they clearly don't think my suggestion is as great as I do.

Monique placed her hand on top of his. "Alex, flowers symbolize fidelity, love, and a fresh start—an amazing future together. I put a lot of thought into choosing these specific flowers for their meanings. And apparently, you were just pretending to listen when I told you about it."

Busted!

"Monie, you know me. When have I ever paid attention to flowers or any conversation about them?"

Monique shrugged. "That's fair."

The server brought their food out.

"Now that it's settled we'll have flowers," Elise cut her eyes at Alex, "let's enjoy breakfast, then head to our first appointment."

***

Alex sat in the back seat of Elise's car as she drove to the first florist.

"There. Up ahead on the right," Elise pointed at the sign at the curb. "T&S Florist."

Since the parking lot was completely empty, she pulled into the space right by the entrance.

"Thorns and Stems Florist?" Monique read the black block letters stenciled on the glass door.

T&S stands for Thorns and Stems?

Elise gave a quick shake of her head and cleared her throat. "Maybe it's a contradiction. Like bad meaning good." She opened her door and hopped out. "Let's check it out."

Monique turned to look at Alex. He shrugged.

"We're here. May as well."

A young woman in her late twenties or early thirties, dressed entirely in black, stood at the front counter and looked up as they entered. Her straight, chin-length bob was dyed jet black, complemented by black lipstick, bold eyebrows, thick mascara, and eyeliner that sharply contrasted her pale, heavily made-up face. She also wore small silver hoops that pierced from her earlobes up to the helix of both ears.

As Alex watched her arrange black roses in a crystal vase, he partly expected her to snip the flowers off, leaving just the thorny stems. Like the name of the shop.

Morticia Addams would be proud.

She placed the shears on the counter. "Hello, welcome to Thorns and Stems. I'm Sable. What can I help you with today?"

Alex and Monique were rooted to their spots. Elise walked forward and extended her hand.

"I'm Elise Daniels. We spoke on the phone yesterday."

Sable nodded. "Oh, yeah. The event planner."

"Actually, I'm a wed—"

"Let me show you the flowers we have now. If you want something specific for the twenty-first, we have just enough time to order it."

Sable led them to the first flower cooler. Alex was surprised at the array of brightly colored flowers, considering Sable's choice of attire.

"Here we have yellow carnations." Sable opened the first glass door.

Maybe this place will work after all.

"They symbolize rejection, disdain, disappointment, and sadness. They're ideal to send to people you dislike or want to break up with."

Or not.

"If you want to send a warning message, orange begonias are a great choice." She picked up a compact, bushy flower with four orange petals in two pairs of different sizes. "Or butterfly weed." She pointed to a reddish-orange flower on a nearby shelf.

Alex sneaked a peek at Monique. Her expression matched his inner thoughts of surprise, disbelief, and slight amusement at the absurdity of the situation. Elise wore a mask of neutrality.

"Then we have the cyclamen, which comes in a variety of colors. We have white, pink, red, and purple in stock." Sable held up a pink flower. Its long stem was topped with petals that reminded Alex of butterfly wings. "These represent a new path in life and separation. So, it's a good flower to send to someone you just broke up with."

All the talk about breaking up and separation made Alex uneasy.

I've got to put a stop to this.

"Um, I don't think—"

"Then there's the black dahlia, which represents betrayal and doom," Sable continued without acknowledging him. "Fun fact. Black dahlias aren't actually black. They're deep maroon, burgundy, or plum that can look black under certain lighting conditions."

He tried again. "That's fascinating, but –"

Sable led them back to the front counter and proudly held up the arrangement she'd been working on when they arrived.

"And of course, the classic dyed black rose, representing death, farewell, and mourning." She placed the vase back on the counter. "So, what kind of event are you planning? A break-up? Divorce party? A defriending?"

Alex speechlessly stared at Sable, unable to decide whether he was disturbed or impressed by her commitment to all things dark and depressing.

Sable's eyes landed on Alex and Monique's clasped hands. "Or are you breaking up with someone else so you can be together?"

Monique shook herself, then broke her silence. "We're getting married. We want flowers for our wedding."

"Married?" Sable looked as if they'd pronounced a curse over her. "Are you sure?"

"Yes!" Alex and Monique said in unison.

Sable turned to Elise with a confused look.

"I'm a wedding planner, not an event planner."

"Oh, I must have misheard you." Sable escorted them to the door. "We don't have anything here for that. But keep us in mind. After all, half of marriages end in divorce."

***

Alex tried to shake off the sinking feeling in his stomach that followed Sable's words, "Half of marriages end in divorce." He knew that all too well and was determined not to repeat his past mistakes.

What mattered more was how Sable's comment affected Monique. She had been unusually quiet during the entire fifteen-minute ride to the next florist, even when Elise tried to engage her in conversation. They needed to talk privately. Until then, he'd have to keep both their minds off the possibility of their marriage ending before it even began.

"Festive Floral," Alex read the sign at their next stop. "Talk about opposite ends of the spectrum."

Monique let out a small chuckle. "Definitely. Although it won't take much for this place to be cheerier than T&S."

Alex opened the door for the ladies, and a tinny chorus of Jingle Bells played from a small box speaker above it. When he crossed the threshold, he stopped in his tracks and blinked uncontrollably. His brain struggled to absorb all the sights and sounds before him. They took Festive Floral very seriously.

The right wall was lined with shelves of poinsettias, mostly in red and white, but also in pink, purple, yellow, orange, and blue. Flower coolers along the left wall were filled with red, white, and green roses.

Didn't know green roses were a thing.

Potted holly bushes and ivy vines were arranged in a display at the center of the room. A small cooler behind the front desk held a large basket of mistletoe bunches. Tinsel, ribbon, silver bells, garland, wreaths, and every other Christmas decoration imaginable were spread throughout the store. It was a bit gaudy for Alex's taste, but Monique wasn't frowning like she had at T&S, so he took it as a win.

Elise approached a woman Alex hoped was an employee, since she was dressed as Mrs. Claus. Not in the stunningly hot Mrs. Claus outfit Monique wore the previous Christmas, but a more traditional look.

"Hi, I'm Elise Daniels. I called about flowers for a wedding on December 21st. Are you Holly?"

Of course, her name is Holly.

"Yes. A Christmas wedding!" She clapped her hands rapidly. "I love Christmas weddings."

Then she's working at the right place.

"You must be the lovely bride," Holly said to Monique, then looked over at Alex. "And this must be your handsome groom."

Holly spun on her heels and headed toward the right side of the shop. "How many poinsettias were you thinking about and in what colors?" Holly stopped walking and laughed. "What am I saying? Your colors must be red and green. Right?"

"Actually," Monique said, "my colors are burgundy and cream, with gold accents."

Holly went pale and swallowed. "Well, yes, I suppose that could work."

"And I'm not having poinsettias," Monique said firmly.

Beads of sweat formed on Holly's brow, and she steadied herself on a nearby shelf. Alex was afraid she would faint. Thankfully, after she closed her eyes and blew out a breath, she regained her perky demeanor.

"Well, you've come to the right place to add some Christmas flair."

"But I don't want—"

"I can see it now," Holly interrupted Monique. "The bridesmaids' bouquets and groomsmen's boutonnieres can be holly bunches." She gestured to the holly display. "Oh, oh, and your boutonniere," she pointed at Alex, "can be mistletoe to match the mistletoe in the bridal bouquet." She winked at them. "Get it?"

"Here is the list of flowers that I picked out. Can you get any of these?" Monique tried again to make her wishes known, but Holly was too far gone in describing her idea to hear.

"It's so clear," Holly had a distant look in her eyes. "Bouquets of holly bunches, complete with berries, and cream roses, tied with a deep red ribbon with gold jingle bells. I'll have to special order the bells. And I'll include the Santa hats and muffs for your bridesmaids at no extra charge."

While Holly looked off into space, apparently seeing her vision, Monique leaned over to Alex and Elise and spoke out of the corner of her mouth.

"How can they carry bouquets if they're wearing muffs?"

Elise slapped her hand over her mouth while her shoulders shook with silent laughter. Alex wondered what a muff was.

"After your final fitting, I can embellish your dress with festive sequins, beads, jewels, and metallic thread." Holly moved her hands in circles as she spoke. "By the way, if you haven't settled on a cake yet, I know a bakery that can make a giant gingerbread house. They can even put an edible Santa's sleigh with reindeer on the roof."

***

"Hopefully, the third time will be a charm," Alex said, trying to stay positive.

Thorns and Stems and Festive Flora set the bar pretty low. The next one had to be better.

At first glance, Petals by Kate seemed normal. The script lettering on the sign and the delivery van in the parking lot suggested it was probably safe to go inside. Alex was happy with the wide variety of colorful flowers, greenery, and ribbons. His worries eased a little. Some.

What's the catch? Is the florist a stern taskmaster? Allergic to flowers? Or some other preposterous thing that I can't think of?

Elise pointed at the white service bell, hand-painted with red, pink, and yellow flowers. "Nice touch, right?"

Alex was cautiously optimistic when, mere seconds after Elise tapped the bell, a woman wearing a pink Petals by Kate polo and jeans came from the back.

"Apologies. I was working on an arrangement being delivered today. You must be Elise. I'm Carly." She extended her hand to Elise.

Elise Shook Carly's hand. "Hi. With me are the bride and groom, Monique and Alex."

Carly became teary-eyed and flashed a forced smile. Alex sensed the window of normalcy was closing, so he jumped in.

"Monique has a list of the flowers we want. Can you take a look at it and—"

Carly shook her head and waved her hands. "I'm sorry." She reached under the counter and pulled out a tissue. "I thought I could do this," she dabbed at her eyes, "but it's just too soon." She dropped her chin to her chest and released a shaky breath.

"My boyfriend and I recently broke up." Her voice trembled and cracked. "He said I was talking about marriage too much. But we'd been together for five years. How much longer did he need to be," she made air quotes, "ready?"

Even though she asked a question, she forged ahead without pausing.

"I mean, really? It was just an excuse to avoid commitment. Don't you think? It just doesn't make sense otherwise. Like last month when…"

While Carly continued her monologue, Alex signaled Monique and Elise to follow him as he eased to the door. Right before he made it out, Carly called out to him.

"Are any of your groomsmen single?"

***

Alex, Monique, and Elise sat at lunch in stunned silence. If those were the best or only options, a wedding without flowers was increasingly appealing to Alex. But the strained look on Monique's face made his heart clench. He grabbed her hand and placed a soft kiss in her palm.

"We'll find flowers, Monie."

Elise nodded vigorously. "Absolutely. Don't worry. Take this off your plate. I'll find a florist who will have exactly what you want, Monique."

"But how?" Monique's voice was just above a whisper.

There had to be more to Monique's mood than just flowers. Was she taking all the unexpected glitches as a sign? Was she rethinking her decision to marry him?

He reined in his spiraling thoughts. No, they were people of faith. These were just minor setbacks.

"Let me, as your wedding planner, worry about that. I have contacts all over the country. Even if I have to fly them in overnight, you'll have your flowers. Okay?"

Monique nodded. "Okay."

***

Alex and Monique arrived at Metropolitan Church much more at ease than they had been before lunch, for two reasons: Thai food and a troubleshooting session.

A delicious meal at Monique's favorite Thai restaurant eased the stress of the florist debacle. After some gentle persuasion, Alex got Monique to open up. While Elise's promise was appreciated, leaving the flower issue entirely up to her was not an option for Monique. So, they called Jessica, Monique's business partner, and found several florists in Atlanta that Jessica offered to contact.

Crisis averted. Kind of.

Alex grabbed Monique's hand. "We make a pretty good team, huh?" His heart raced at the sight of her smile, and he was convinced it always would.

"Yes, Alexander, we do. Ready for our next session?"

"No doubt, Monie Love."

***

Pastor Mike rose from one of the wingback chairs when Alex and Monique walked into his office. Pastor Olivia nodded at them from the other chair.

"Alex. Monique. Come on in. Please close the door behind you and have a seat." He motioned to the couch.

After Pastor Olivia prayed, Pastor Mike started.

"Last session, we talked about something old—family heritage and traditions. Today, our topic is something new."

"The new item represents optimism and hope for your future as a couple," Pastor Olivia explained.

Wait, didn't Monique say that flowers represent a new beginning and a future together?

He tilted his head slightly toward Monique and saw she had turned hers toward him. They were thinking the same thing. During the session about something old, his dad "lost" his antique cufflinks. When the topic was something new, they had an issue with the flowers.

I pray this isn't a pattern. If it is, this is going to be a long ten days.

"While you can't predict the future, the two of you should be on the same page about where you're headed," Pastor Olivia continued. "Or recognize the areas where you need to come to a compromise."

"So, for today's activity, we'll ask you some questions, and each of you will write your answers on these cards." Pastor Mike handed each of them a stack of twelve letter-sized cardstock sheets and a marker.

"Like the Newlywed Game," Monique said.

"Yes," Pastor Olivia answered." But unlike the Newlywed Game, you're answering for yourself, not what you think your fiancé will say. It's vital that you be completely open and honest. This is concerning your future as a couple. Don't give the answer you think you should give. But the raw, uncut truth. Are you ready?"

Alex had no doubt that they were. After all, they'd been through a thorough pre-marital counseling program and had talked about all the significant issues.

This should be a breeze.

Alex grew more confident with each answer he wrote down. There weren't any controversial or sensitive topics. When Pastor Mike asked what excited them about marriage, Alex broke into a wide grin. Monique must have sensed it because she shot him a glance.

"Don't you dare," she whispered through her teeth.

But that only made his smile broader. "Pastor Mike, Monique is trying to keep me from being completely honest, like you said."

"Really?" Monique whispered.

Pastor Mike chuckled. "Be honest. But keep it PG."

After they wrote their answer to the last question, Pastor Mike took their markers.

"I'm surprised there wasn't a question about finances," Monique said.

Pastor Olivia shook her head. "Oh, there's an entire session dedicated to that."

Great.

"Now you're going to share your answers," Pastor Olivia said. "Your homework will be to talk through those areas where your answers differ the most. You ready?"

"Yes," Alex and Monique answered in unison.

"Okay. Where do you want to be twenty years from now?"

They had already talked about retiring to part-time work by sixty-five, so they could travel more. Just as he was about to complain to himself again, he changed his attitude.

Since we have to do this, I may as well make it as enjoyable as possible.

As expected, they breezed through questions on setting the temperature for the air conditioner and heater, merging their daily routines, where they would live, and their career goals.

"What excites you about marriage?" Pastor Olivia asked.

Alex flipped over his card. "Waking up next to Monique every day."

"Aww," Monique rubbed his arm, "that's sweet."

"What did you put?"

She showed him her card. "Building a life with you."

Pastors Mike and Olivia looked at each other and smiled.

We should be done in about ten minutes.

"What concerns you about marriage?" Pastor Mike asked.

"Being a good husband."

He'd messed up once, and he'd be lying if he said he wasn't concerned about doing so again.

"What about you, Monique?" Pastor Olivia asked.

"Being a good wife."

Alex was surprised. *Why would she think she wouldn't be?*

"If by 'good' you mean mistake-free, you've set an impossible standard," Pastor Mike said. "Everyone makes mistakes. And you will most likely inadvertently do things that hurt or disappoint your spouse. The key is to communicate, make necessary adjustments, and forgive."

Alex knew he was right. There was no such thing as a perfect person, but the idea of hurting Monique made his stomach turn.

"How will you sign your name as a married couple?" Pastor Olivia asked.

Alex thought that was the most trivial of all the questions, but he answered it anyway.

"Alex and Monique Patterson."

Of course.

Monique stiffened, then, after a beat, flipped her card over. "Alex Patterson and Monique Lovelace-Patterson."

Alex sat straight up.

What?

"Lovelace-Patterson? You want to hyphenate?"

"Yes." She spoke carefully, but firmly.

He leaned back on the couch, his eyes never leaving her face. "I… didn't know that was the plan. We never talked about this."

"We never talked about it because you assumed I'd just drop my maiden name."

"Why?" *Is she not all in?*

"Lovelace is who I've been my whole life, Alex. It doesn't disappear at the altar. And I've accomplished a lot professionally as Monique Lovelace. So, I want to keep it. Is that a problem?"

Alex lifted one shoulder, but he couldn't shrug off the feeling that there was something more to it. Pastor Mike gently raised a hand before he could speak.

"Hold up. I hear both of you. Alex, you're worried that this means Monique isn't fully committed to this marriage. Monique, you're worried you'll lose part of yourself if you don't hold onto your name. Those aren't small issues, and they won't be solved in two minutes on this couch."

Pastor Olivia leaned forward, her voice kind but firm. "Put it on your homework list and talk through identity—how to be one without erasing the two people God brought together."

"At least she doesn't want to name your first child after her high school sweetheart." Pastor Mike looked at Pastor Olivia out of the corner of his eye.

Alex's mouth hung open in disbelief.

Pastor Olivia nudged Pastor Mike with her knee. "Mike, stop. You're going to make Alex hyperventilate." She turned her attention to Alex and Monique. "It was just a suggestion. And it wasn't *after* him. Brandon is just a nice name."

"Okay, let's keep going. We have two more questions to get through," Pastor Mike said. "What is something your fiancé does that you pray that they never stop?" Pastor Mike asked.

"Being supportive," Monique answered.

Does that include supporting hyphenating?

"Being my friend."

Monique grabbed his hand and squeezed. "Always, Alexander."

"Alright, that brings us to our last question." Pastor Olivia looked down at the index card in her hand. What is something your fiancé does that you pray they will stop doing today? Monique?"

She flipped her card over. "Comparing things to his first marriage."

Alex winced and shook his head. "I don't do that all the time. The few times that I do mention it, it's saying what we're doing is better."

"Not when we were deciding cake flavors for the wedding."

"That wasn't a *comparison*. I said, 'Last time we had red velvet, and the guests loved it.' I was being helpful." He looked to Pastor Olivia for support, but she just shook her head.

"Quit now before you get further behind, Alex."

Pastor Mike chuckled: "Son, let me help you out. Erase the word 'first' from your vocabulary unless it's about Corinthians, Thessalonians, or the like."

"Got it." He turned to Monique. "I never meant to upset you, but I can understand how it would. I don't like hearing about whatshisname from your past, so it's fair for you to expect the same from me."

Monique nodded. "Thank you. And don't worry," she put her hand on his knee, "I'll help you remember."

Her stern tone and expression convinced him beyond any doubt that she would.

"Alex, your turn," Pastor Olivia said. "What does Monique do that you pray she'll stop?"

He flipped his card over. "Shutting me out when she's stressed."

Monique's brow shot up to her hairline. "Shutting you out?" She turned to face him. "When do I –"

"Like today at lunch. I had to practically stand on my head to get you to even talk to me about our flower situation."

"Flower situation?" Pastor Olivia asked.

"Don't ask," they said in unison without breaking eye contact with each other.

"You talk to Jessica before you talk to me," Alex said.

"Jess and I are in business together."

"You and I are in life together."

Monique opened her mouth, but no words came out. After looking at Alex in silence for a few moments, she leaned back on the couch.

Pastor Mike cut the tension in the air in a firm, gentle voice.

"Okay, okay. These answers might sound different, but they're actually similar. Monique, you want to know this marriage won't live in the shadow of the last one. Alex, you want to know you're allowed inside when things get heavy. You just identified the second topic for your homework: trust and presence."

Pastor Olivia smiled at them warmly. "Don't worry. You did well. Your answers revealed where some real conversations need to happen. And you'll probably have to discuss these topics more than once. The homework isn't about winning or getting what you want. It's about seeing where you're not hearing each other yet."

Alex and Monique looked at each other and nodded. He grabbed her hand and squeezed it. His heart soared when she squeezed back.

We can do this. Right?

***

After a light dinner, Alex and Monique decorated the condo before settling on the couch in front of the television. Alex turned on a screensaver of a roaring fire. They created a cozy Christmas vibe, but the counseling session still hung in the air.

Alex faced Monique and broke the silence. "So… Lovelace-Patterson?"

She turned to him, put her elbow on the back of the couch, and rested her cheek on her fist. "Yes. Lovelace-Patterson."

He pondered his words before he spoke. "I just… I thought marriage meant we'd be one. Same team, same last name."

"And I thought marriage meant bringing all of me into it. My name is part of that, Alex. I've worked for it. Lived with it. It's not just a name—it's me."

He tried to understand, but it still wasn't clicking. "So, you don't think taking my name means commitment?"

She met his eyes. "I don't think keeping my name is a lack of commitment. Commitment is about being there for each other every day. I'm not less committed to *us* just because I don't want to lose *myself.*"

Alex let her words sink in. Then he sighed and ran a hand over his face. "I didn't realize it was that deep for you. I guess I wanted a clean slate." He cracked a small smile. "You know, no shadows from the past."

Monique threw a throw pillow at him. "Nice try, Alexander, and not the same thing." She softened. "But maybe the slate isn't meant to be wiped clean. Maybe it's meant to hold both of our names, both of our stories."

Alex let out a slow breath. *I'm trying to get there, sweetheart.*

"And you'd still be able to call me Monie Love."

He nodded. "Monie Pat does sound weird."

"Our names being slightly different won't stop us from being there for each other."

"Tall words from someone who shuts me out."

She held his gaze. "You're right."

I must have fallen asleep and am dreaming.

"I'm sorry. What did you say?" He cupped his ear.

She nudged his shoulder. "You're right. I do."

She dropped her head, closed her eyes, and took a deep breath. When she looked at him again, her eyes were clear and open.

"I'm used to figuring things out on my own. And with He Who Shall Not Be Named…well, let me just sum it up by saying I've never had a relationship partner I could trust with my struggles. Someone who'd help find a solution that's best for me." She put her hand on his cheek. "Until now."

Alex thought his face would crack from the strain of his wide grin.

"I have to reprogram my default. So, I won't get there overnight, but I'll keep working at it until I do."

"Don't worry, Monie Love. I'll help you remember."

She shook her head. "Alexander Patterson, what am I going to do with you?"

"I have several ideas, but first, can we talk about the elephant in the room?

She sat cross-legged. "It's weird, right? Something old. Your dad loses the antique cufflinks."

"Well, they weren't really lost."

"I know, but still. Then on the day we talk about something new, there's an issue with the flowers."

He'd had the same thought earlier. "What's next?"

"Something borrowed."

He squinted. "You don't owe money to the mob, do you?"

"Not unless you consider the mortgage industry the mafia."

He wagged his head. "I could go either way depending on the day."

"You haven't borrowed anything from anyone for the wedding, have you?"

"No."

Other than the cufflinks. Which Dad didn't offer to me when I married Bri—

He stopped before he could say his ex-wife's full name. Just in case Monique could read his thoughts.

"Good. And blue isn't one of our colors."

He sat up. "Wait a minute. We're being ridiculous. We don't believe in superstitions."

"No," Monique agreed, "but God does use circumstances to get our attention sometimes."

Between the flowers and the two counseling sessions, God already had Alex's full attention. What more could there be? But he'd think about that later.

"Now, back to what you're going to do with me."

Chapter 4: Both
Something Borrowed

Tuesday, December 10 — 11 days until the wedding

Tuesday morning, Monique pulled into the Metropolitan parking lot, uncertain why she felt the need to arrive thirty minutes before their last counseling session with Pastors Mike and Olivia. 'Compelled' was probably too strong a word. Her early arrival was likely due to her early waking, which resulted from restless sleep.

She and Alex ended the evening on a good note, but the underlying issues—identity, trust, and presence—still lingered between them. While it wasn't realistic to expect everything to be resolved after just one conversation, she couldn't shake the anxious feeling in her stomach.

Would they make it to the altar?

Monique entered through the Fellowship Hall rather than the administrative office building. Metropolitan was known for its beautiful Christmas decorations.

Maybe seeing their displays will improve my mood.

She took a breath at the sight of a twenty-foot Christmas tree in the lobby, which confirmed her decision. Its vibrant, royal-blue branches were elegantly adorned with various shades of silver and white globe ornaments. Strategically placed crystal icicle ornaments and fairy lights made it shimmer and glow.

Wow.

After circling the tree to admire its full beauty, Monique continued down the hall toward the administrative offices. Movement in one of the rooms drew her attention. She peeked inside and saw Pastor Olivia, impeccably dressed and poised even as she arranged chairs.

Hashtag goals.

"Good morning, Pastor Olivia."

She looked up and checked her watch. "Hi, Monique. You're here early."

Monique nodded. "Yeah, I, um, got an early start. But it gave me time to see some of the decorations. The tree in the lobby is gorgeous."

"Thank you." Pastor Olivia walked over to her.

"Are you joining our session today?"

Pastor Olivia smiled warmly and nodded. "Yes. You did well yesterday, you know. Those counseling sessions aren't supposed to be easy."

She half-laughed and shook her head. "Well, yesterday definitely wasn't. Alex looked like I knocked the wind out of him."

Pastor Olivia gestured for Monique to have a seat, then sat beside her. "You just gave him something he didn't see coming. Men tend to think they've got the playbook figured out. Surprise throws them off."

Monique sighed. "I wasn't trying to throw him. I just… I don't want to lose myself in being his wife."

Pastor Olivia nodded slowly. "A good marriage doesn't erase who you are—it expands it. You and Alex have to realize that."

"We did our homework and made some headway. But we each have more work to do."

Pastor Olivia rested her hand lightly on Monique's arm. "Whatever you decide to do, just know that your name doesn't make you any more or less of a wife. And don't let anyone tell you otherwise."

Monique nodded.

"But don't forget—Alex isn't just asking about a name. He's asking if you're all in. Find a way to show him you are, hyphen or not. Letting him help when you're struggling shows your full commitment to the relationship."

The knot in Monique's stomach untied "Thank you, Pastor Olivia. I needed that."

Pastor Olivia looked at her watch and stood. "Come on. Let's head over to the office. I'm sure the men are there by now."

Monique put her handbag on her shoulder and followed Pastor Olivia out of the room, wondering what more was in store for her and Alex at their next session.

***

Pastors Mike and Olivia sat in the wingback chairs

across from Monique and Alex. Monique was surprised at how quickly she had gotten used to the couch in Pastor Mike's office. Even though there had only been three sessions—and challenging ones at that—she was going to miss the place.

"The topic for this last session is Something Borrowed," Pastor Mike said.

This should be easy since we haven't—

"It's not about loaned money or possessions," Pastor Mike continued.

Never mind.

"The purpose of the item was to borrow happiness or blessings from a happily married person," Pastor Olivia explained. "While it's a nice thought, each couple and, therefore, marriage, is unique. The overarching tenets of love, honor, respect, fidelity, and so on apply to all, but how they are demonstrated varies for each relationship."

Pastor Mike made eye contact with Alex and then with Monique. "One of the most detrimental things you can do is compare your marriage or spouse to another."

Monique could wholeheartedly agree with that. She disliked it when Alex talked about his previous wedding. If he ever compared her to Brionne... it would be a bad day in the Lovelace-Patterson household. She glanced at Alex out of the corner of her eye. He sat upright and looked straight ahead.

Is that a bead of sweat on his forehead?

Pastor Olivia handed Monique and Alex a writing

pad and a pen. "So, today's activity has to do with silent expectations."

Alex's brow furrowed. "What are silent expectations?"

"They're those things that you assume your spouse will do because they're 'no-brainers,' 'obvious,' and 'normal,'" Pastor Mike explained. "We all have them, and we all go into relationships with them. Usually, they're borrowed from other relationships we've seen or experienced."

Ah, there's the "something borrowed."

Pastor Olivia picked up the discussion. "We subconsciously tend to act and expect according to what we saw growing up – good or bad. The problem is that we grew up in different households, so our experiences were different. And therefore, what we expect is as well."

This is a lot. Maybe I won't miss being here after all.

"So, Monique, you may do what you saw your mother do. And Alex, you may do what your father did."

"But my dad is a great husband. And Monie's mom is a great wife. Why is that not okay?"

Pastor Olivia smiled at them, indulgently. Like one would with a five-year-old who insisted they would be a dragon when they grew up.

"Because the assumption is that Monique will respond to you like your mother responds to your father. And that you will respond to Monique the way her father responds to her mother. But your father and

Monique's mother aren't married to each other. And they aren't the two of you." She pointed at them to emphasize her point.

Pastor Mike studied their faces for a moment, then spoke.

"Let me give you an example. I expected Olivia to have dinner ready by the time I got home from work every day, just as my mother had for my father."

"Wait," Alex held up his hand and shook his head, "what's wrong with that?"

Does he expect that of me?

"There's nothing wrong with the expectation itself. The problem is that I hadn't discussed it with Olivia first. So, when she wasn't doing it, tension surfaced."

Pastor Olivia placed her hand on Pastor Mike's knee. "I knew he was upset about something, but didn't know what. When it finally came to a head, we argued about it, got it out in the open, and were able to address it."

"And we didn't stop there. We discussed how our daily life would flow to prevent arguments. About that at least."

They laughed and briefly bumped shoulders.

They make it look so easy, when what they're saying is anything but.

"How can we talk about things we don't even realize are there?" Monique asked.

Pastor Olivia shrugged. "Some things you won't realize you expected until they're unfulfilled."

Monique turned to Alex to see if he looked as exasperated as she felt. His eyes were wide and glazed over.

Yep, he is. At this rate, we're never going to pass these sessions. Then they will refuse to officiate, and we won't be able to get married.

Screams of frustration lodged in the back of her throat.

Maybe this is a sign.

She quickly shook off the negativity and refocused on Pastor Olivia. No, Pastor Mike had started talking at some point.

I hope I didn't miss anything major.

"As children, we assume that every household is like our own. As we get older, we realize that's not true, but we don't have a lot of real-life examples of any other way to do it."

Monique adjusted her posture, wondering when the couch had become so uncomfortable. Since Alex had been her best friend, she figured she knew all about him. However, it was becoming clear that knowing Alex as a friend and knowing him as a husband were two very different things.

So much for marrying your best friend being the solution to a happy, lasting marriage.

"We're going to start you off," Pastor Olivia said. "Again, the purpose of this session is not to identify every silent expectation you have, but to recognize some of the most common ones so you can spot others when they come up and know what to do." She pointed to the notepads and pens Monique and Alex were holding. "On the first page is a list of topics."

Monique flipped open her notepad and reviewed the list: chores, division of labor, childcare, frequency of intimacy, time spent together, and time spent apart.

"Write down at least one silent expectation—things that you assume will happen automatically—for each topic. Share what you wrote with each other. Then have an open discussion without judging what your partner wrote, and come up with helpful solutions."

Monique's expectations didn't seem that outrageous to her. But she supposed that was the point. Things that were obvious to her might have never even occurred to Alex.

She hazarded a glance at Alex. He wrote swiftly, fully focused on the task at hand. Then he looked up at her, winked, and smiled.

Her heart fluttered.

Maybe we'll be okay.

***

Monique balanced the box with the bridesmaids' gifts on her knee as she rang the doorbell at her parents' condo at The Well. The door swung open, and her mother pulled her in for a hug, as much of a hug as she could with the box in the way.

"Hi, sweetheart." Naomi closed the door. "Richard, Monique is here."

"Hey, baby bird!" her father called from his recliner

in the great room.

"Hey, Dad."

Monique turned to her mother. "So, would you rather do bridesmaids' gifts or the seating chart?"

Naomi grabbed the box. "Gifts. Without question. No way I'm answering to Cousin Millie about where she gets seated."

"Chicken."

"Yep."

Monique followed her mother to the craft room. "Can't say I blame you. Who RSVPs for six people?" She sighed and shook her head.

"Thankfully, Elise is handling it, while I ignore Cousin Millie's calls and texts."

Monique silently said a prayer of thanks for Elise. Besides handling unconventional RSVPs and seating requests, she was managing the wedding favors, programs, contacting the ushers and hostesses, finishing the place cards, and finalizing the guest count for the caterer.

But not the bridesmaids' gifts. Monique insisted on buying and assembling them personally. They were the women who were closest and dearest to her. She wouldn't be where she was in life without them.

"In each tote bag, include a sachet of foot soak, a pair of memory foam slippers, a scented spa candle, a set of satin scrunchies, and the personalized insulated tumbler. The tote bag has their initials on it, so you know which tumbler belongs to which person," Monique instructed.

Naomi nodded. "Got it."

They worked in silence until Monique couldn't keep the questions bombarding her mind to herself.

"Mom, how did you know for sure that Dad was the one?"

Naomi kept working without making eye contact. "I don't think anyone knows for absolute sure."

That was not the response I was expecting.

"Really?"

Her mother nodded again. "You only know at the time, because you change and your spouse changes."

"Pastors Mike and Olivia said something similar."

"The key is to grow and change together." Naomi put a candle in Yvette's tote bag, then looked up at Monique. "Why do you ask?"

Monique dropped a sachet in Tara and Desiree's totes, then heaved a sigh. "We've only had three sessions, but each one has revealed things I didn't realize about him. Or myself."

"That's good."

"Good?"

Alex and I may be on the verge of breaking up, and my mother thinks it's a good idea.

"Yes. The biggest fallacy about marriage is that when you find 'the one,' everything will be easy." She took Monique's hand in hers. "The truth is, you find the one that you're willing to work through all the tough spots with. And as you conquer each one, you get closer and closer. And your relationship gets better and better."

Monique shook her head. "Some experts say marriage to the 'right' person is easy. Others say marriage is hard. Which one is it?"

Naomi smiled as she watched Richard pass the craft room on his way to the kitchen.

"Both."

***

Aromas of cinnamon, cloves, ginger, and nutmeg floated to the craft room just as Monique and her mother finished the last bridesmaids' gift. Her dad had started making hot cider. Eggnog and hot cocoa would follow.

She chuckled to herself. *My dad is the Christmas beverage king.*

She made her way to the kitchen to join him.

"Hey, baby girl. You wanna help your old dad make cider?"

She wrapped her arms around his waist and lay her head on his shoulder. "You? Old? Never."

He placed a peck on her forehead, then nudged her with his shoulder. "Start cutting the lemon. I'll do the apples."

As Monique deeply inhaled the fresh citrusy scent of the sliced lemon, her thoughts drifted to the counseling sessions. She would have been lying to herself if she said she wasn't concerned.

How were there so many unknown things coming to the surface, less than two weeks before the wedding?

Had she ignored signs with Alex like she had with Justin?

Maybe it's me. Perhaps I'm just not wife material like Justin said.

It pained her to think that Justin was right.

Maybe I need another man's opinion.

She watched her dad core apples for a few moments before starting a conversation about wedding preparations. They laughed about Thomas pretending to lose the cufflinks and the odd florists she'd visited. She ignored the tightening in her stomach at the reminder that they still didn't have a confirmed florist and eased into the topic that was really on her mind.

Monique kept her gaze on the cutting board as she talked about the counseling tensions, as if they were harmless stories rather than the heavy worries that kept her awake at night.

"We've talked, of course, but…" She paused, searching for the right words. "I mean, *you* wouldn't have questioned mom's commitment just because she wanted to hyphenate."

She let the words hang, hoping the weight of the rock that formed in her gut didn't carry over in her voice. Richard laid the paring knife aside and studied her. She forced herself not to squirm under his assessing gaze.

"Monique, whether I would or wouldn't is irrelevant."

She opened her mouth to protest, but her father raised his hand to stop her.

"Not only are we two different people, but we're also in two different stages of life. You can't even compare me at thirty-nine with him now. I was married and had three young children at that age. Alex is just starting to build his family and wants a strong foundation for it."

"I hadn't thought about it like that."

She wanted to build a life with Alex. Had her insistence on hyphenating made him doubt that?

"Don't compare Alex to me or expect him to be me. That's not fair to him or your relationship. He's the man you're marrying, not me. Love all of him. Even the parts you don't like or disagree with."

"Thanks, Dad." Monique wrapped her arms around him again, and he returned the embrace.

"Why is keeping the Lovelace name so important to you?" he asked into her hair.

"It's who I am and always will be. As Alex and I become one in marriage, I want to stay true to myself. I don't want to get lost in the shuffle. I need to know that I can still be the woman I've become."

He stepped back just enough to look in her eyes, while keeping his arms around her shoulders. "Have you explained that to Alex?

She shrugged. "Not in those exact words."

"Then use those exact words. He needs to know that you're not one foot in and one foot out, ready to escape at a moment's notice if things get hard. Because they will get hard. Alex knows that from experience."

It occurred to her that Alex was probably as sensitive about his previous marriage as she was. She didn't want to be compared to it. He didn't want to repeat it.

"A man wants to know that he has the heart of the woman who has his. Does Alex have yours?"

Tears sprang to Monique's eyes. He did—wholly and completely. Always would and probably always had, which was why their conflicts were so concerning.

Because if they broke up, he'd take her heart with him.

***

Alex was disappointed when he arrived at his parents' house and saw that his father's car wasn't in the garage. The important talk with the man he admired most would have to wait. He rang the doorbell, then used his key to go inside. His mother was in the big room, comparing the Merry Memphis Christmas schedule with the family calendar.

"Hey, Mom."

"Hi, sweetheart."

He bent at the waist so she could kiss him on the cheek.

"Where's Dad?"

"At the barbershop."

I need to get on Sean's books for my haircut, so I'll stop by there next. And maybe catch Dad.

He dropped onto the sofa and sighed.

"That sounds way too heavy for a man about to marry the love of his life."

He debated for a few moments whether to tell his mother what had been happening. Once he was sure that his mother would side with him, he opened up.

"Monique wants to hyphenate. You would never do that, Mom."

Imogene took her glasses off and set them on the side table.

"That's neither here nor there, Alex. For a number of reasons. First, you're not marrying me. You're marrying Monique. She's not me, and she's not her mother."

Just what Pastor Mike said.

"And things are different now. Your father and I got married much younger than you and Monique are. We were in our early twenties. Just kids, really." She shook her head and smiled wistfully. "Although you couldn't tell us that at the time."

Granted, Monique taking his last name was a silent expectation. But it wasn't just his name. It was like she didn't want… him.

His mother leaned forward and looked him in the eye. "Let me ask you this. Is her hyphenating enough to make you want to call off the marriage?"

He jerked upright. "No, of course not."

She tilted her head. "Then maybe it's not as important to you as you think. Maybe your real concern is what other people will think about her hyphenating."

He flinched at the sting of truth in his mother's words.

She held his gaze a moment longer, then put her glasses back on and went back to planning the Patterson holiday festivities.

Everyone seemed to share the same opinion, but Alex still wanted a second, technically fourth, opinion.

Someone has to agree with me.

***

The scene at Final Cutz was familiar and comforting to Alex. Clippers buzzed in the background of the debate over who would win the Super Bowl. The older men laughed and trash-talked over a domino game in the corner.

Sean tilted Thomas' head to line him up, then placed a warm towel on his face. Alex made eye contact with Sean in the mirror, and they exchanged head nods.

"You need an appointment for the big day?"

Hopefully, there will still be one.

"Yeah. Next Thursday or Friday."

"Okay. Text me a day and a time, and I'll make it happen."

Thomas got up from the chair and walked over to Alex. "Hey, Son."

Alex pressed send on his text to Sean. "Hey, Dad."

Thomas studied Alex's face, then pointed to two empty chairs across the room. They walked away from the other barbers and patrons and took a seat.

"You've had that storm cloud on your face since yesterday. May as well tell me what's bothering you."

He looked around, then quietly asked, "What if Mom wanted to hyphenate?"

"What?"

Finally! Someone on my side.

"Monique wants to hyphenate her name. Lovelace-Patterson. I just… I didn't see that coming. Felt like she was saying she's not all in."

His father's familiar low chuckle rumbled in his ears.

"Mm. I hear a whole lot of Patterson pride. And I know it well because you got it from me." Thomas shook his head and laughed again.

Alex frowned. "You think I'm wrong for wanting her to take my name?"

"No, son," he said softly. "There's nothing wrong with wanting it. But you need to ask yourself—what does that name really prove? That she's yours? That she's committed? You already know she is, or she wouldn't be sitting in pre-marital counseling with you."

"It just feels like…" Alex swallowed the word on the tip of his tongue, not wanting to admit it.

I've come this far, and if I can't tell my dad, who can I tell?

"It feels like rejection."

Thomas nodded. "Have you told her that?"

He shook his head. "I didn't really realize it until just now."

"Tell her. I can't read her mind, but I know she doesn't want you to feel that way. She probably just wants acknowledgement of who she was and is as the two of you write your new story together."

Alex slowly processed the new information.

"So, you're saying it's not a threat to us?"

He put his hand on Alex's shoulder. "I'm saying a name on paper doesn't make or break a marriage. Hyphenated and non-hyphenated people get divorced."

Don't I know it.

"But what you do every day really matters. The way you listen when she's scared, the way you stay when it's tough—that's what shows her she's safe. If you keep that your focus, you'll stop worrying about her email signature."

Alex cracked a smile. "You know about an email signature?"

Thomas grinned. "Please, I've forgotten more than you've learned."

He genuinely laughed for the first time in what felt like weeks, but had barely been a day.

"Son, your mom and I have been married for over forty years. We've been talking, arguing, and learning the whole time. That's marriage. Now, if you want to last that long, don't fight to win the name game. Fight to win her heart every day."

Alex sat back in the chair, feeling lighter and more convinced that he and Monique could make it work.

***

Late Tuesday evening, Alex stood at the front door of Monique's parents'—no, brother's—house. This conversation with Monique needed to be face-to-face, not over the phone. Seconds after he rang the doorbell, the door swung open, and Monique stood before him.

She is beautiful.

Although she was probably going for a casual, comfortable look, her natural beauty was on full display, with glowing skin, bright brown eyes, and full, curved lips…

"Alex?" Monique peered at him.

He blinked rapidly to pull himself out of the trance she'd put him in. "Huh?"

"Are you coming in?"

"Oh, yeah. Right. Sorry."

As they walked through the house to the back porch, Alex noticed that the downstairs was unusually empty and quiet, with no sign of RJ, Yvette, or the boys.

"Where is everybody?"

Monique shook her head and half-smiled. "When I told them you were coming over, suddenly everyone had 'things to do' upstairs."

A slight smile touched Alex's lips. While he was fairly sure their conversation would end well, he was glad they wouldn't have an audience on the off chance that it didn't.

Alex grabbed two throws from the basket near the door and stepped out onto the back porch into the chilly December air. The string of Christmas lights hanging in the sunroom glowed faintly through the window, providing a soft backdrop.

They sat down, and the memory of the last time they were on the swing flickered in Alex's mind. It was from December the year before—the night they foolishly broke up. Alex was determined not to make the same mistake again.

They sat in silence for a few moments, then Alex spoke.

"I talked to my parents today. They said a name on paper doesn't make or break a marriage. It's how we show up every day that matters."

Monique stared at him wordlessly with wide eyes. Then she shook herself.

"Pastor Olivia and my dad said almost the same thing. That my name doesn't make me less of a wife. But also, that you're just asking about a name—you're asking if I'm all in."

He held his breath, waiting for her next words.

Monique took his hand and spoke with a soft, steady voice. "I am all in, Alex. Even if I hyphenate. I need you to believe that."

He laced his fingers with hers. "I also need you to let me in—even when you're stressed, even when you're scared. Not shutting down. Not preparing to leave."

"I'm not. I committed to us, but I don't want to lose myself in the process."

He nodded. "I'm beginning to understand. But honestly, it may never make complete sense to me. Can you accept that?"

"I can. Besides, I still don't understand why you have one pair of black and gold Jordans for high school alumni events and another pair of the exact same style black and gold Jordans for college alumni events."

It's so obvious.

"It's like this—"

She held up her hand. "Please don't."

Their laughter eased the tension in the air. As they swung in silence, Alex was lost in thought. Finally, his soul settled, and his resistance softened.

"So… Lovelace-Patterson?"

"Lovelace is who I was born. But Patterson is who I'm choosing." Monique placed her hand on his cheek. "You're not losing me, Alex. You're gaining all of me."

He exhaled slowly. "Lovelace-Patterson, it is."

The porch grew quiet again, and a shared sense of peace wrapped around them beneath the glow of Christmas lights. He draped his arm over her shoulders and pulled her close. "I love you, Monie Love."

She rested her head on his shoulder. "I love you, Alexander Patterson."

Alex tried to take the win and move on, but they hadn't talked about the silent expectations from the session that day.

Maybe we can skip that exercise.

He wasn't in the mood for another disagreement because each one was more intense than the last. He hoped that their breakthrough would make the next discussion easier.

Only one way to find out.

"Now, about those silent expectations…"

Chapter 5: Alex
Something Blue

Wednesday, December 11 — 10 days until the wedding

Alex's doorbell rang just as he shrugged into his overcoat.

"I thought we were meeting at Pastor Reginald's office." He checked his watch. "Maybe she brought me some of Mom Naomi's hazelnut coffee."

He smiled and walked to the door. "Or maybe she just couldn't wait to see me. I do have that effect on her."

Alex opened the door in anticipation, then froze. Neither Monique nor her mom's coffee was on the other side of the door.

"Lisa, what brings you by?"

She held up a box wrapped in glittery red paper, tied with white ribbon, and topped with a green bow. "It's your Secret Santa gift, silly. I got your name." She smiled and lightly shook the present.

"Um, I didn't sign up for Secret Santa this year since I'm not based in the Memphis office."

"Oh," she shifted her weight from one foot to the other. "Your name must have been added by mistake. Well, anyway," she thrust the box at him, "enjoy!"

He reluctantly accepted it, concerned that someone would be gift-less because of the mix-up.

"Thanks. Mind if I open it later?" He joined Lisa on the walkway, then closed and locked the door behind him. "I have a pre-marital counseling session in twenty minutes."

He headed to his— his and Monique's—truck. Lisa walked beside him, then used her key fob to unlock the sedan parked next to him.

"Counseling? Are you and Monique having problems?"

Why does she look happy? I'm being ridiculous. That's just her regular expression.

Alex shook his head and waved his hands. "No, no. Nothing like that. Our pastors here wanted the opportunity to meet with us before officiating the wedding."

"Oh. Yeah. That makes sense." Lisa nodded. "Sure, you can open it later. But let me know if you like it."

"Of course. And thank you again."

He tossed the little wrapped package on the console and got in the truck, but stopped before he fully closed the door. "Hey, let me know if someone gets left out because of the mix-up."

She tossed her hair over her shoulder and shrugged. "I'm sure everything will be fine, but I'll check into it. And don't forget to let me know if you like it."

It's a Secret Santa gift. Those are notoriously lame.

"Will do. See you later."

***

Alex parked beside Monique in the Grace Life Church parking lot. She signaled for him to keep the engine running, then jumped out of her car and got in the passenger's seat.

"Brrr! The temperature dropped overnight." She pointed at the gift on the console. "What's this?"

He'd almost forgotten it was there.

"Lisa dropped off a Secret Santa gift just as I was leaving."

She raised her eyebrows. "You signed up for Secret Santa this year?"

"No," he shook his head, "that's just it. I don't know how she got my name."

She grinned, reaching for the package. "Can I open it?"

"Knock yourself out. It's probably a mug with something about not talking to me until I've had coffee."

Again, lame.

Monique shook the box a few times, then tore into the wrapping. Tissue paper crinkled until her hands stilled. Her mouth opened. Then closed. Then opened again.

Alex glanced over. "What is it?"

She held up a pair of silky navy-blue boxers with his initials monogrammed in silver thread on the waistband. The green bow from the wrapping floated gently from Monique's lap and landed on the floor mat.

He choked.

"What in the—? How—? Why—? That is not—" he sputtered. "That's… not a mug."

Monique stared at the fabric pinched between her fingers like it was a filthy rag. "This is not festive, Alex. This is… intimate. Why is Lisa giving you underwear?" Her voice grew louder.

He groaned and smacked the steering wheel. "I don't know! I thought it was chocolate or socks or something."

Monique forcefully stuffed the boxers back in the box, then tossed the offending object in the back seat. "Lisa is officially uninvited from the wedding."

"Monie…"

She cocked her head to the side and pinned him with a look he knew all too well.

Alex opened his mouth to argue, then closed it again. They'd just brokered peace with hyphenating and silent expectations the night before. No way was he going to start a disagreement over a gift he didn't want from a high school classmate that he only stayed in touch with because they were work colleagues.

"You're right. There's no defending it."

She looked at her watch. "It's time to go in."

Monique got out of the car without waiting for Alex's response and closed the door firmly. She didn't slam it, but Alex got the message.

***

Alex and Monique checked in at the front desk and were shown to the counseling room. Moments later, Pastor Reginald joined them.

"Alex, good to see you." He gave Alex a clap on the shoulder. "And Monique," he took her hand in his, "we miss Alex in the Men's Ministry, but he made the right choice to be with the woman he loves."

Monique smiled and slightly blushed. "Thank you, Pastor Reginald." Her eyes shone with affection when she briefly looked at Alex

Yes! Thank you, Pastor. You're helping a brother out.

Pastor Reginald gestured to one of the two loveseats facing each other. "Please have a seat."

Monique and Alex sat, and Pastor Reginald folded his tall, lean frame on the loveseat across from them.

"How were your first three sessions?"

"Eye-opening," Alex said.

"Challenging," Monique said.

"But good," they said in unison.

"Great." He clasped his hands together. "Today's session will finish out the poem. You did, something old, something new, and something borrowed. So, today's topic is Something Blue."

"Funny you should mention something blue," Monique murmured.

Alex hung his head.

"What was that?" Pastor Reginald asked.

Alex widened his eyes at Monique, then turned to Pastor Reginald. "Nothing, nothing. Please continue."

Pastor Reginald looked between them a few times before resuming.

"The color blue represents fidelity, love, and purity. It's where the term 'true blue' gets its origin. The blue object represents faithfulness to your spouse. We'll explore three questions today."

He handed each of them a piece of paper with three questions printed on it.

"How will you proactively prevent situations that might lead to temptation? What are your thoughts on your spouse having close friends of the opposite sex? And how do you establish boundaries with friends of the opposite sex?"

Monique snorted.

"Monie, come on," Alex pleaded softly.

"Okay, that was definitely something." Pastor Reginal said. "What's going on, you two?"

Alex sighed. "My co-worker, who is also our high school classmate, dropped off what she said was a Secret Santa gift this morning."

"But he didn't sign up for Secret Santa," Monique added.

Pastor Reginald frowned. "You didn't?"

Alex shook his head.

"Huh." Pastor Reginald folded his arms across his chest. "Continue."

"I figured it was just a mix-up since I usually participate. And while I'm not based in the office here, I do come back with some regularity."

"But you digress." Pastor Reginald motioned for

him to get to the point.

Alex nodded. "Right. I threw the gift in the car. When Monie got in, she asked if she could open it, and I told her yes."

"And…?"

"And," Alex swallowed as heat crept up his neck, "it was a pair of blue silk monogrammed boxers."

The silence in the room was deafening.

Pastor Reginald leaned back on the loveseat and steepled his fingers. "So let me get this straight," he said slowly, eyes flicking between them, "on your way here, Alex's coworker gifted him… underwear?"

"Monogrammed boxers," Monique corrected crisply. "Like she's claiming territory."

"I don't know if I'd go that far…" Alex started.

Monique turned to fully face him. "No one buys you boxers without wanting to see you in them."

"She's not wrong," Pastor Reginald added.

Alex flushed even more.

I can't believe I'm having this discussion with my pastor!

But he was grateful that it was Pastor Reginald, who was only about ten years his senior and more like a peer, rather than Pastors Mike and Olivia, who were his parents' age. If this had come up in one of their first three sessions, he would have prayed for the ground to swallow him up.

Alex groaned and dragged his hand over his face. "I told you, I didn't know what it was. I had no idea she'd ever do anything like that. Or think that it's okay to do so."

"And I told him Lisa is uninvited from the wedding."

Pastor Reginald pressed his lips together as if he were fighting back a laugh. "Well, I will say this is a first. Most couples come to me with arguments over money or in-laws. You two brought me… boxers."

"How could I have known?"

Monique tapped his knee. "Remember last year when you applied for the position you have now in Atlanta?"

Of course, he remembered. "Yeah. And?"

"Remember how Lisa texted you about the Senior Account Manager position that might be opening up in Memphis? You even said it was out of the ordinary for her to text you like that."

The penny dropped. Alex's mouth hung open, but no words came out.

Oh, boy.

Monique folded her arms across her chest and crossed her legs. "Handle it."

Pastor Reginald nodded solemnly, though his eyes twinkled. "This is perfectly aligned with today's topic. Boundaries," he said, tapping his tablet with the stylus. "Every marriage needs clear boundaries. Who's in your inner circle? Who gets a say? Who does not get to buy your man underclothes?"

Alex slumped lower. "I'm never living this down."

"Correct," Pastor Reginald said matter-of-factly. "But you are going to learn from it. Alex, you have to be vigilant about guarding this relationship. Sometimes that means being clear with people who may not have the best intentions. And Monique, part of trust is believing him when he says he had no idea. You two have to work together on both fronts—setting boundaries outside, and giving grace inside."

"Monie, you know I didn't do anything to encourage that. Right?"

She sighed and softened. "Yes. I know that. I trust you." She lifted a finger. "However, I don't trust Lisa." Monique turned to Pastor Reginald. "I'll give him grace. But Lisa is still off the guest list."

Pastor Reginald chuckled, scribbling something in his notes. "Well, Sister Lisa will be fine watching the livestream."

Can't argue with that.

"This was a good discussion. Now for your homework—"

"Besides dealing with Lisa?" Monique asked.

Alex dropped his chin to his chest. Pastor Reginald tried to hide his smile.

"Yes. It's really prep work for tomorrow's session. You have to work together to complete two projects today. One that Monique leads and Alex supports, and one that Alex leads and Monique supports."

He was interrupted by the receptionist buzzing him.

"Apologies. I'm needed up front for something urgent. I'll be back shortly."

Alex just wanted to talk about anything other than the gift that turned into a curse from Lisa.

"Did you decide where you want to take the bridesmaids and groomsmen for dinner tonight?"

"You know what? I'm tired of eating out. We should cook. A home-cooked meal says a lot, don't you think?"

Alex shrugged. "Sure, as long as by 'we' you mean 'you.' You know I can't boil water."

Monique laughed. "Two amazing cooks and an actual chef in your family, and you have no cooking skills. How?"

"Someone has to be the official taster. And it didn't stop you from falling in love with me?"

He winked, and she smiled.

"True, and you know I'm a sucker for the underdog."

"Excuse you. I'm the one to beat." He thumped his chest.

"You are." She gave him a kiss on the cheek.

"And while you're cooking, I'll change out that showerhead and replace the toilet flapper in the guest bathroom. No need to pay a handyman for such an easy job. All you have to do is—"

"All I heard was '*wah, wah, wah.*'"

He chucked and put his arm around her. "That's ok. You're really pretty."

She gave him a playful shove just as Pastor Reginald walked back in.

"Ok, thanks for waiting." He sat down, smiling broadly.

Too broadly.

Why do I have a bad feeling about this?

"Monique, you'll take the lead on the plumbing repairs, and Alex, you'll prepare the meal for your dinner party."

Alex and Monique sat in stunned silence while Pastor Reginald continued to smile at them as if he hadn't caused another wedding fiasco.

He must have listened in on our conversation. Is the room spinning?

They launched into a protest.

"But our dinner for our friends will be ruined!" Monique patted Alex's shoulder. "No offense, honey."

"Oh, none taken." Alex faced Pastor Reginald. "And so will the plumbing at the condo!"

Alex turned back to Monique to apologize, but she spoke first, nodding her head rapidly. "Yeah, you're right."

"Great. You're both motivated to do a good job and help the other do a good job."

Pastor Reginald raised his hands before they could launch into their counterarguments.

"You each have the skills for the other to succeed. You must listen—really listen—and follow their directions. And when it's your turn to give directions, be as patient and understanding as you want them to be with you."

When he put it like that, it was hard to argue.

"Good. We're all on the same page." Pastor Reginald said, apparently taking their silence as a sign of agreement.

"So, to recap. First, let me say that this was an excellent session. Alex, you need to set boundaries with Lisa—sooner rather than later."

As soon as I leave here, as a matter of fact.

"Then you both have projects to complete outside your area of expertise that carry significant consequences. But if you trust each other and work together, I have no doubt you'll be successful."

He stood and walked them to the door. "Oh, by the way, the person giving directions has to have their hands tied behind their back. Have fun and see you tomorrow."

Pastor Reginald closed the door to the counseling room, leaving Monique and Alex in the hallway.

Alex turned to Monique, who looked as shellshocked as he felt.

Well, at least we're on the same page.

***

Alex stopped in the doorway of Lisa's office, rapping lightly on the frame. She glanced up, surprised but clearly pleased.

Don't get too happy.

"Alex, hi. I guess you wanted to let me know how you feel about the gift in person." She tucked her hair behind her ear. "Please, have a seat."

"Yeah." He stepped inside, keeping his tone even. "This won't take long, and I'd rather stand."

Lisa smiled and tilted her head. "I know it was a little personal, maybe, but—"

"Way too personal," Alex cut in, his voice steady.

Her smile faltered. "What's that supposed to mean?"

"Lisa, I need you to hear me on this. That gift crossed a line. We don't have that kind of relationship."

"Everyone needs a work wife to talk to, vent to, collaborate with, have inside jokes, and support them." She looked hopeful.

"My real wife is woman enough to be everything that I need, want, and dream of. And more."

She huffed. "You're not married yet, Alex."

"In my heart, I am, and either way, not to you. Besides, this isn't the first time you've tried to interfere."

"What are you talking about?"

He exhaled slowly. "Remember last year, when you texted me about that opening in Memphis? At the time, I thought you were just being helpful. But looking back, I realize you weren't encouraging me professionally. You were trying to keep me here."

Lisa blinked, then tried to recover with a laugh. "I was just looking out for you. You've got history here, roots. I thought you'd be happier in Memphis than running off on some ill-conceived—"

"Running *to* Atlanta," Alex corrected firmly. "Because that's where Monique was. And she's my future, Lisa. Not Memphis. Not whatever you were hoping for."

Color rose in her cheeks. "Alex, you're reading too much into this. The boxers were a joke. The text was a favor."

"No," he said, shaking his head. "They were boundary crossings. And they have to stop.

Her face softened. "Remember that night in high school when a group of us went to the park? We talked all night. We bonded."

Alex didn't remember that night the same way. It was a group conversation about what they wanted to do with their lives.

"Lisa, that was over twenty years ago. And we just talked. Like I talked to everyone else who was there."

"Why was it always Monique?" She stood to her feet and dropped the pretense. "Even when you had a girlfriend, you never let go of Monique. And she never really saw you or appreciated you."

He'd had enough of the conversation.

"You don't know what Monique did or didn't do, nor is it your concern. Look, I respect you as a coworker, but that's all. There's no room for anything more. And I won't let you cause trouble in my relationship or my wedding."

Lisa's lips pressed into a thin line. "So, I'm just what? Not welcome?"

He met her gaze without flinching. "You're not invited to the wedding, no. That's a day for the people who've supported Monique and me. And this," he dropped the unwrapped box with its contents on her desk, "isn't support. It's confusion. And I won't have any more of it."

Silence stretched. Lisa crossed her arms, looking away. "Well. I guess I got my answer."

"Yeah," Alex said quietly. "You did."

He left before she could say anything else and pulled out his phone as he walked down the hall. By the time he got to his car, he'd sent Monique a one-word text: Handled.

Alex parked in front of his condo in the spot next to Monique's SUV. He had everything they needed from the home improvement store. All Monique had to do was make a few simple repairs, and all he had to do was cook a delicious meal for their closest friends to show their appreciation for the time and money they spent on their wedding.

No pressure there.

He grabbed his bags, got out of the truck, and went inside. "Honey, I'm home!"

Monique's laugh drifted from the kitchen and wrapped around his heart.

"Just in time for lunch."

They decided to devise a game plan for the rest of the day while eating. But he had to fess up first.

"While I was getting the stuff for the repairs, I thought about just doing them and telling Pastor that I need to work on relinquishing control and learning how to support." He ate another forkful of his burrito bowl, his conscience clearer.

"Same," she admitted. "But we committed to going through the counseling, so we can't cheat. We're not even halfway through yet."

"Yeah, and come on. We rise to challenges every day in our careers and businesses. Surely, we can put the same, if not more, effort into our relationship."

"Exactly. We can do this," Monique affirmed.

"So, which do you want to do first?

"Repairs, so if I mess them up, you'll have time to fix them before everyone gets here."

"It'll be fine."

Alex chose not to mention that he bought two of everything needed for the repairs, just in case.

***

Alex stood in the guest bathroom with his hands behind his back as Monique tied his wrists with gold ribbon that, until a few minutes earlier, had wrapped a box of peppermint bark. She pulled him toward her until the backs of his legs touched a barstool. After he was seated, she stood in front of him wearing old sweatpants, one of his t-shirts, and…

"What's with the Santa hat?"

She jingled the ball on the end of her cap. "It puts me in a festive mood."

"We're doing repairs on an investment property, not decorating, Monique. This is serious."

She jingled her hat again. "Maybe that will help your heart grow three sizes, Mr. Grinch."

Christmas music drifted from the living room. Mariah Carey hit her high note like she was cheering for Monique. He blew out a breath and looked up at the ceiling.

"This is cruel and unusual punishment, having to sit by while someone else destroys my perfectly good plumbing."

Monique placed her hands on her hips and gave him a look. "Correction: while someone else heroically fixes your plumbing." She pointed at him. "You're supposed to tell me how to do it. Give good instructions, and you'll get good results. So, Professor Patterson, start teaching."

Poor choice of words. Many of his college professors were not good instructors.

"Fine. Step one: pick up the adjustable wrench." He used his chin to point in the tool's general direction. Fortunately, it was enough for Monique.

"This one?" She grabbed it and shook it.

"Not a hammer, Monique. Don't swing it."

"Whatever. What now?"

"Turn the screw to open the jaws wide enough to fit around the shower arm."

"Done."

"Now, put it on the shower arm, just behind the showerhead. Then turn it counterclockwise. Gently."

She climbed into the tub, braced the wrench, and tugged. Nothing happened. She tugged harder. The whole shower arm groaned. He winced and wriggled against his restraints.

"It's stuck." Her eyes held an unspoken request for help when they met his.

Alex hadn't expected such a challenge not to act. Initially, he thought tying his hands was overkill. But as he watched Monique struggle and fought the urge to fix it for her, he understood the need for the restraints.

He exhaled to slow his heart rate. "Smaller turns. Slowly. Lefty loosey, not Hulk smash." He hoped the reference to her favorite movie universes would have a positive effect.

"Ha ha," she muttered through a slight smile. With a grunt, the showerhead loosened, nearly slipping from her hand. "Got it!" She held it up like a trophy. "See? Plumbing prodigy."

"Yep, you're dangerous," he said. "Now wrap the Teflon tape around the threads."

"This little white ribbon?"

"Yes. Clockwise. If you go the wrong direction, it'll unravel when you screw on the new showerhead."

She narrowed her eyes. "You're just making that up to sound technical."

"Trust me. Go the wrong way, and we could end up sitting in a flooded bathroom."

"Fine." She carefully wrapped the threads, then twisted on the new showerhead. "Like this?"

"Tighter. Use the wrench to get a snug fit, but don't overdo it."

"Define 'overdo it.'"

"Breaking my wall and owing me a new bathroom."

She tightened the connection, then hopped out of the tub. "Moment of truth." She turned the knob. Water poured in a smooth stream. Her jaw dropped. "Yay, me! It works!"

Alex grinned. "You go, Josephine the Plumber. Now for the toilet."

Monique eyed the tank warily.

"All right," Alex shifted in his seat. "First, take off the tank lid and set it gently on the towel. Emphasis on gently."

She searched the items he'd laid out on the bathroom floor. "Where are the gloves?"

"What gloves?"

"I'm not touching the inside of a toilet without gloves," she protested.

"You replaced the showerhead without gloves."

"Showers are used to getting clean. Toilets are used to—"

"Fine. I think there are some gloves under the sink in the kitchen."

Monique left and shortly returned with gloved hands. "Ok. I'm ready. Do what now?"

"Take the tank lid off and set it *gently* on the towel," he repeated.

She lifted it with exaggerated care. "Relax. I'm not a barbarian."

"Debatable."

She stuck out her tongue, then leaned over the tank. "Okay, now what?"

"Unhook the chain from the flapper—the rubber piece at the bottom—then remove it."

Monique wrinkled her nose but reached in. "This is gross. They should make latex opera gloves so that I can be covered to my elbows."

"Keep going," Alex urged. "Now put in the new flapper. Then clip the chain on the same spot."

The chain clinked as she fumbled. "It's too short."

"Move it down a link or two. You want enough slack so the flapper closes completely, but not so much that it tangles or gets caught under the flapper."

"Listen to you, Toilet Whisperer," she teased, finally clipping it in place.

"Now test it. Push the handle."

She pressed the handle with her elbow. Water whooshed, refilled, then settled with a healthy gurgle.

"Yes!" She took off the gloves and threw them in the trash.

"You did it!"

"*We* did it." She scrubbed her hands and forearms with five pumps of soap and hot water.

"You're right. My instructions were brilliant," Alex added smugly. "Untie me so I can take a victory lap."

"Not a chance." Monique shook her hands over the sink, then dried them with a towel. "Maybe I should leave you tied up and do some more home improvement. Didn't you say something about a backsplash in the kitchen?"

"Lord, give me strength," Alex muttered, but the corners of his mouth curved upward.

***

Two hours later, the movie credits scrolled on the TV screen. Monique looked at her watch, grabbed the remote, and turned off the TV.

"Okay. We've got to get started, or dinner won't be done before our guests arrive."

Alex groaned. Cuddling on the couch with Monique outshone almost all other activities, especially cooking, which he never did. Ever. His parents and sister had given up on him decades ago. And Kendra was an executive chef. So, what made Pastor Reginald think Monique could succeed where professionals had failed?

"I considered stacking the deck in our favor with spaghetti," Monique confessed. "Boil the noodles, brown the meat, sauce from a jar, and salad from a bag. But that's not the kind of meal we want to serve their closest friends and family. Is it?"

"Maybe not. But your logic is solid. And the meal would be edible." Surely, she wasn't expecting him to prepare an elaborate meal. "They'll forgive us if we explain the situation."

She placed a hand on his knee. "Hear me out. There are many countertop appliances that make cooking a great meal easier. So, it's basically measuring the ingredients, putting them in the appliance, choosing the function, and setting the timer."

"And I own none of them."

"True," she nodded, "but between my mom and your mom, we have them in duplicate." She gestured for him to follow her into the kitchen.

"An Instant Pot, rice cooker, air fryer," she pointed to the silver and black objects on the counter, "and a multifunction oven."

"Whatever you say."

"Exactly. That's the homework. You just do what I say."

His brows drew together in concern. "Why are your eyes twinkling?"

"Because I'm in love?"

He snorted. "Yeah, right. I think it has more to do with telling me what to do and my having to obey."

"Well, there's that." She pulled him over to the counter, where the appliances and raw ingredients were. "We—correction, you—are doing Instant Pot marry me chicken—"

"How appropriate."

"Yellow rice in the rice cooker, air fryer roasted vegetables, mixed green salad, and take-and-bake Texas Roadhouse yeast rolls."

He didn't even attempt to return her smile. "How about I do the salad, and you do the rest?"

"It'll be fine."

She used the exact words he had. He hoped that she had a backup plan, too.

***

Monique sat perched on a barstool, her wrists tied neatly behind her back with a red ribbon she'd picked herself. She looked far too comfortable for someone in "support mode."

Alex bent at the waist and carefully read the labels for every button and knob on the appliances. "What are these supposed to be pictures of? Why couldn't they have used their words?"

"You'll do fine. Just follow instructions."

Did she really believe that, or did she say it because she thought she should?

He stood up straight. "Okay, what's first?"

"Take the package of chicken thighs out of the fridge, rinse them off, then pat them dry."

After rinsing the chicken under cold water in the sink, Alex grabbed a roll of paper towels and wrapped his hand several times. It might have been too many, but he figured it was better to be safe than sorry. He placed a chicken thigh in his towel-covered palm and squeezed.

"Like this?"

When Monique didn't answer, he looked over his shoulder. Her lips were tucked in, and she shook with silent laughter.

"You're supposed to be helping, Monie."

"Your way is… original, but it's getting the job done. Once you dry all the thighs, pour the olive oil in the Instant Pot and press the sauté button."

Now, that I can do.

"Next, season both sides of each thigh with salt, pepper, garlic powder, and paprika. Oh, and get under the skin, too."

He glanced at the spice rack and groaned. "There are twenty jars here. Which one is paprika?"

"The one that's red and says paprika."

He remembered his father saying that food should be "well-seasoned," so he sprinkled the spices generously—too generously. A cloud of pepper shot up his nose. He quickly turned to sneeze and bumped the counter.

Time seemed to slow down. The tray slipped off the counter. Monique's eyes widened as she jumped off the stool and ran toward him. Alex quickly spun around and caught the tray just before it—or any of the chicken—hit the floor.

His heartbeat thrummed in his ears, and his hands shook slightly.

"Whew! Quick hands, Alexander," Monique said between heavy breaths.

"Thanks, but I'm almost sure cooking isn't supposed to be this hazardous."

"You'd be surprised." She walked back over to her stool and sat. "Now that we're both awake, put the chicken in the Instant Pot and brown each side for two or three minutes."

"Which one?"

"Which one, what?"

"Two minutes or three minutes?"

"You don't have to be so…" She stopped. "Three minutes, Alex. Brown each side for three minutes."

"Thank you. That is a specific direction that I can follow."

After the chicken was successfully browned, Alex added the remaining ingredients, set the Instant Pot to pressure cook, and started the timer. For the first time, he thought dinner might not end in disaster.

"Nice work," Monique said. "Now, measure two cups of rice."

He dumped dry rice straight into the pot.

"Wait, you're supposed to rinse it first."

"Wash rice? It's not lettuce."

"Unless you want glue, rinse and drain the rice until the water's clear."

He grumbled but did as he was told. Water spilled onto the counter as he swirled the bowl of rice and water. When he tried to drain it, he tipped the pot too much, and half the rice went straight into the sink.

Uh oh.

He looked at Monique, but she just smiled.

"Check in the cabinet to your left. There's another bag of rice. Use the colander when you drain next time. Then add the seasoning."

After Alex rinsed, drained, and seasoned the rice, he set the rice cooker. He plopped down on the stool next to Monique.

"I need a nap."

She chuckled and nudged him with her shoulder. "You're doing great, and you're almost finished. Only the roasted vegetables need to be prepared. The yeast rolls go straight into the oven, and the salad is already ready."

He slapped his knees. "Then I'd better get to cutting veggies."

Except for having to go back and cut some of the initially large pieces into smaller ones so they would "cook evenly," prepping the vegetables was incident-free. They also had just enough time to shower and change before the chicken was done.

***

Monique joined Alex in the kitchen just as the Instant Pot beeped. She immediately went back into instructor mode, even though her hands were free.

"You have to release the steam before you open the lid." She handed him a long-handled wooden spoon. "Use this to turn the stem release valve to the venting position."

He took the spoon from her. *Is she punking me?*

"Is this really necessary?"

"Only if you don't want a face full of scalding steam."

Alex toggled the valve and jumped when the steam whooshed out in a jet.

"Is it supposed to do that?" he yelled over the noise.

"Yes, ergo the spoon."

As if on cue, the air fryer beeped, and smoke curled from the basket. The ding of the rice cooker and the buzz of the oven quickly followed. Alex and Monique worked together to get the food onto serving dishes—familiar-looking dishes.

"Is this my parents' tableware?"

Monique nodded. "Uh-huh. They were very supportive of your first attempt at a dinner party."

He chuckled. "Probably more like surprised, incredulous, and worried."

She smiled. "Those, too."

He surveyed the plates of steaming chicken, fluffy rice, and roasted vegetables that covered the counter. Everything looked good, but that was only half the battle. He cut off a small piece of chicken.

"Moment of truth." Alex took a tentative bite, then froze. "Wait. This… this is good."

"Told you," Monique leaned on the counter with her arms crossed. "All you needed was the right coach."

They put all the food and place settings on the table.

He sighed to ease the nervousness. Soon, their closest family and friends would be subject to his cooking. "Here goes nothing."

She touched his arm. "You already know the meal is good. Relax and enjoy."

"You're right. And we have a working guest bathroom." He looked down at her. "We make a pretty good team, if I do say so myself."

"Good thing since we're going to be together forever."

He pulled her to him for a kiss, but the doorbell interrupted him. So, he settled for a peck on the cheek.

As they walked to the door, a thought occurred to him.

"Wait! What about dessert?"

"Your mom provided that. Said she'd made one too many cakes."

"Oh? What kind did you get?"

Monique smirked. "Red velvet."

Alex laughed and got in another hug before opening the door.

I love this woman.

***

Alex relaxed on the couch with his arm around Monique. Even though one of his favorite movies was on, he replayed the evening in his mind.

After the wedding party had dug in, the room had settled into holiday and wedding chatter. Plates were scraped clean, laughter lingered, and somehow no one had complained about the food.

He released a long exhale.

Monique lifted her head from Alex's shoulder and looked up at him. "You realize everyone went back for seconds, right?"

Alex blinked and shook his head. "After all the chaos—"

"Dinner was actually a hit," she finished for him, smiling softly.

"Not too shabby, soon-to-be wife."

"Not shabby at all, soon-to-be husband."

"I have another confession. I bought extra parts in case something went wrong with the bathroom repairs."

She shrugged. "That's okay. While I was at Texas Roadhouse, I bought a family meal as a backup."

He sat straight up, causing her to fall sideways. "What? I didn't see anything in the fridge."

"That's because it's at Stacey's house." She grabbed his arm, and he helped her sit back up. "I planned to text her if I needed her to bring it."

He laughed. "That was a smart move."

Monique put her hand over his heart. "We're a smart move."

Alex covered her hand with his. "The smartest and best move I've ever made."

What a day!

A gift of underwear. A counseling session. A tough conversation. Plumbing work. And a dinner party.

Tomorrow has to be easier.

Chapter 6: Monique
To Have and to Hold

Thursday, December 12 — 9 days until the wedding

The next morning, Monique and Alex sat side-by-side across from Pastor Reginald, regaling him with stories from the night before.

She leaned forward and spoke with her hands. "First, the showerhead attacked me, and the toilet tank," she shivered, "just the thought of touching it was gross. And he," she thrust her thumb at Alex, "didn't think I needed gloves."

"That's nothing. She brought in so many gadgets that the kitchen looked like an appliance store." His knee brushed against hers with every movement he made.

She smiled and bumped his shoulder. "Stop exaggerating."

He used his fingers to tally the items. "An Instant Pot, a rice cooker, and an air fryer. And I still had to use the oven. Who does that to a person who doesn't cook?"

Alex rested his arm on the back of the loveseat behind Monique. Pastor Reginald's shoulders shook with laughter.

"Sounds like you had quite a night."

Monique absentmindedly looped her finger around

Alex's. He softly rubbed the back of her hand with his thumb.

"We did," they said in unison.

"Good. Last night's projects served as prep for today's topic, which is the first part of the traditional wedding vows: to have and to hold. It's a promise to belong to each other exclusively and to watch over, protect, and support one another."

Pastor Reginald continued. "Most people think of the word 'have' as indicating ownership or possession. And to a degree, it does. But to have also means, 'I got you' and 'I'm here for you.'"

Monique tilted her head and focused more intently. *I'd never thought of it that way.*

'To hold' also has multiple meanings. It can mean holding someone in your arms for comfort, protection, or to surround them. It can also mean supporting or sustaining something. Additionally, it implies staying by their side, regardless of the circumstances.

Pastor Reginald leaned forward and rested his elbows on his knees. "Monique, when you were doing the repairs, did you feel supported, directed, or dictated to?"

She took a moment to gather her thoughts.

"I'd say directed, but not in a bad way. I hadn't thought about, let alone done, any plumbing work before. So, I needed clear directions." She shifted impossibly closer to Alex. "And Alex gave directions in a guiding way rather than commanding. So, I felt safe to ask questions, to get it wrong, and to get it right.

Don't get me wrong, there was plenty of teasing and jabbing." She looked into Alex's eyes. "But I think that was to get me to relax. So, yeah, I felt supported."

Alex spoke softly to her. "Did it work?"

She nodded and touched her forehead to his.

"Alex, what about you?

Monique jumped as Pastor Reginald's voice penetrated their bubble. She'd forgotten he was there.

"I was nervous and completely out of my element. I was on edge and worried I would ruin the dinner we'd planned as a thank you to our closest friends," he admitted.

She snapped her head back at Alex. "Really?"

He nodded.

"I couldn't tell."

He lifted one shoulder. "I can hide my feelings sometimes. Good or bad."

That's true. At the cookie party last year, I thought he was completely unbothered. Until a kid named Henry showed up.

"So, Alex, did you feel supported, directed, or dictated to?"

"Definitely supported. When I almost knocked the chicken on the floor, she ran over to help, even though her hands were tied and she wouldn't have been able to do anything."

"I'd actually forgotten they were tied at the time."

She had instinctively jumped into action to help and save dinner.

"And when I accidentally poured the first bag of rice

down the drain, she just smiled and told me where to find another bag."

"It wasn't the whole bag. Only half," she explained to Pastor Reginald. "And dinner turned out great. Everyone went back for seconds."

Alex tried to hide his smile and, if Monique wasn't mistaken, he blushed a little.

"You both shared how you felt about doing something unfamiliar. But what about the opposite? How did knowing how to do the task but being unable to make you feel?" Pastor Reginald asked.

Monique shifted uncomfortably at the memory. She'd maintained a calm face for Alex, but inside, she was screaming and had to force herself to stay on the stool, except when the chicken was about to hit the floor. All bets were off then.

"That was even more uncomfortable than being out of my element. I try to be as efficient as possible. It would have been quicker and easier for me to cook than to explain each step to Alex. So, it was counter to my usual method." She rolled her shoulders. "It made me itch."

Alex chuckled and nodded. "It was really tough for me to watch Monique struggle. My instinct was to jump in and fix it. I'm supposed to make things right for her." He paused. "But if I had, I would have robbed her of the chance to be successful – or at least try."

"That's good. Often in marriage, the harder, less comfortable choice is ultimately what's best for the relationship." Pastor Reginald's gaze warmed, then sharpened slightly. "But what happens when the mess isn't a toilet or a pot of chicken?"

He didn't push too hard, just let the question linger. Silence hung in the air for a moment. Monique's smile faltered, and Alex's shoulders tensed.

"Homework's easy when it's minor repairs and recipes. The tougher part is naming the things that could trip you up later." He looked at Alex. "Like how Monique wants you to support her in her business." He then shifted his gaze to Monique. "Or how Alex wants you to support him on his career path and investments."

He leaned forward. "While the question is essentially the same, what support looks like for each of you varies. Just like with your projects last night. That's where the other part of the pre-work comes in – communication."

That's why our hands were tied. To make us use our words.

For communication to work well, what you say needs to be clear to the listener. It might seem obvious to you, but if the person you're talking to doesn't understand, you haven't communicated effectively.

Monique fought the urge to fidget and plastered on her professional smile.

"You each have two tasks. First, tell the other what you need to feel supported. Second, give the other person what they need, not what you need. Then you'll truly have and hold each other."

But what if you're afraid of how they will react to what you say?

Alex's reaction to hyphenating was a surprise.

What if we can't come to an agreement the next time?

Pastor Reginald looked at his watch. "Oh, good. We have time for one more exercise."

Maybe I should fake a headache so we can leave without arguing.

"Have either of you made a significant commitment to someone else that could affect your life together that you haven't already discussed?"

She inwardly laughed at herself for worrying. *We've talked about all the—*

"Uh, maybe?"

Monique slowly turned to face Alex. "Excuse me?"

He rubbed the back of his neck. "I'm named as Miles' guardian if anything happens to his parents."

She was speechless. Briefly. "Why am I just hearing about this?"

He shrugged. "I didn't think about it until now. Besides, it's only in the event that both Barrett and Chanelle pass away, and neither set of grandparents can take him."

She pinched the bridge of her nose and hung her head. "I can't believe you never mentioned this before."

"It's not something that regularly comes to mind, Monie. I mean, who wants to think about two of their closest friends tragically dying at the same time?"

"I get that, Alex. I'm just surprised it never came up, considering the class we took in Atlanta, all our talks about the future, and the sessions and homework here."

Pastor Reginald intervened. "I can understand, Alex, how you wouldn't want such a horrible event in your thoughts—"

"Thank you, Pastor. That's why—"

"But," he stopped Alex's defense, "you should talk through it. Soon. While we pray that the circumstances never occur, fulfilling this commitment would drastically change your life overnight. Your first conversation about it shouldn't happen when you've suddenly become parents."

Ugh.

The conversation about becoming parents was a sore spot for her.

But Alex didn't know.

Oh, they had talked about starting a family, and she honestly said she wanted children. Monique had wanted kids for years. One reason she worked so hard to make things work with Justin was because she wanted to start a family before turning forty. But there she was, thirty-nine and just getting married.

Maybe.

While intellectually she knew that hundreds of thousands of women had uncomplicated pregnancies and healthy babies at forty and older, it didn't silence the questions in her mind.

Was she too old? What if she can't conceive? What if it's declared too risky?

Would Alex have and hold her then?

And don't even get started on running a business with small children.

She tuned back in just as Pastor Reginald brought his prayer for them to a close. Alex squeezed her hand. She pressed his back and added her own prayer that their relationship would survive premarital counseling.

***

Moments after Monique and Alex arrived at Elise's office that afternoon, Elise greeted them in the reception area and led them to the client consultation room. After some light refreshments, they took their seats at the oval table for a wedding update.

Although Monique wrestled with concerns and doubts in other areas, she hadn't wavered in her choice of Elise as her wedding coordinator. She never even considered anyone else. After all, Elise's work was flawless. She had offices throughout the Southeast, including Memphis and Atlanta, and she was an Empower PR client.

"Let's get down to the reason you're here." She angled her laptop so that Monique and Alex could follow along. "Don't worry about taking notes or remembering all of this. After we finish, I'll email everything to you."

"Thank you." Monique sat back in the chair and exhaled.

One less thing to do.

"Your final RSVP count is… drumroll, please."

Alex patted the table top.

"One hundred ninety-five. I gave the caterer and the Peabody a count of 200 to give ourselves a little wiggle room. And we're still under our estimate of two hundred twenty-five."

"That works for me. Alex?"

"Yep."

Elise reviewed the seating chart, then showed them the place cards, programs, and wedding favors. After they checked the list of final vendor payments, Elise confirmed the transportation arrangements to and from the Peabody, where the wedding and reception would take place.

Everything was exactly as Monique wanted. Some even better.

Maybe the wedding isn't doomed after all.

She looked over at Alex and suppressed a laugh. He was trying to feign interest, but his eyes were glazed over.

He's probably thinking about tonight's football game.

"You are going to love the enlarged engagement photo that will be displayed next to the sign-in table."

Elise reached behind her chair and placed a twenty-three-inch by seventeen-inch poster on an easel that Monique hadn't noticed until then. A smile came to her lips as she took in the image before her.

She wore a flowing, burgundy knee-length dress with a halter neckline, round collar, and a cinched waist. Alex donned a cream polo shirt with a burgundy-stitched logo and tan dress pants that fit as if custom-made. His hair and beard were trimmed to perfection.

Alex is *quite handsome, if I do say so myself.*

But the moment the photographer captured was the most striking.

Slightly bent at the waist, her eyes were closed, and her hand rested on her chest just below her neck as she laughed at a private joke Alex had said loud enough for only her to hear. He smiled and looked down at her, his eyes filled with love and adoration.

"It's perfect," she whispered.

"It is," Alex agreed.

"Glad you like it," Elise said. "And speaking of the sign-in table," she placed another box on the table and pulled out the items one by one.

First was a clear, fillable ornament the size of a fishbowl with a gold removable cap.

"Your guests can sign their names or write short messages on one of these," she held up packages of burgundy, cream, and gold strips of paper, "and drop them in the ornament. We have pens with ink of each color, so they can mix them up."

"I like it," Alex said. "It was hard for me to picture it when Monique

described it, but I get it now."

"Good. Now, you pick up your dress," she looked at Monique, "and your tux," she looked at Alex, "tomorrow. Please make sure you have a reminder in your phone."

They both verified the location, shop hours, and name of the person to ask for.

"If I send you a reminder in the morning, don't take offense. It's my job to overcommunicate. You both have a lot on your plates, so it's easy for things to slip through the cracks."

Elise swiped her tablet screen. "All the bridesmaids have their dresses, and the groomsmen have their tuxes. That brings me to the last item I have for today. The tasting for the rehearsal dinner is scheduled for Monday, the 16th, at 1:00 PM." She tapped on her phone. "I just sent you the meeting invite with the location and directions."

Their phones pinged seconds later.

Alex shook his head and chucked. "I can't mention it to my folks. They insisted they could do the cooking, but I want them to relax and enjoy the weekend."

Monique nodded her agreement.

"We're all on the same page then. Any questions before we wrap up?"

One topic was blaringly absent from Elise's update.

"And the florist?" Monique asked.

Elsie didn't hesitate. "I've connected with Jess, and we're making headway."

"But no one is confirmed yet."

Alex reached for Monique's hand, and she let him take it in his.

"Correct, but we're very close. In fact, I have a call with Philoma, your original florist, later today."

Why didn't she lead with that?

"So, she's going to be available after all?"

"Well, no, but she can get me in touch with Blooms by Bethany."

They're just flowers. The wedding can go on without them. They're just flowers. The wedding can go on without them.

Monique took a deep breath, then checked in with herself.

Nope. The knot in my chest is still there.

"Okay, well, we'll keep praying about it."

Elise reached across the table and lightly tapped Monique's hand with her finger. "What did you tell me when I was freaking out over opening the office in Jackson, Mississippi?"

One corner of Monique's mouth lifted. "To trust the process and the plan."

Elise nodded. "You also told me that you wouldn't have encouraged me to branch out if I couldn't handle it, that you had my back, and that you weren't going to let me fail."

Monique swiped a tear from her cheek.

"Now, I'm telling you, Monique. I have you back. You will have the flowers you want at your wedding." She paused. "Do you trust me?"

Monique nodded, and the knot dissolved.

Thank you, God, for surrounding me with amazing people.

"Then off you go." She shooed them away. "I'm sure you have some homework or some kind of follow-up from your counseling session."

Thanks for reminding me.

***

As Alex helped Monique in the truck, she could tell he had something on his mind. Most likely because Else mentioned counseling homework. When he pulled out of the parking lot onto the street, her feeling was confirmed.

"Monie, I wasn't trying to hide the guardian thing from you. Honest. I truly didn't think of it until this morning when Pastor asked."

She sighed. "I know, Alex, and I get it. If I were named as guardian for one of The Crew, I'd feel the same way."

His shoulders dropped, and he smiled.

"And to be clear," Monique continued, "I don't have a problem with it. Miles is a sweetheart."

Even if Miles wasn't a great kid, she'd still be all in. Having a family with Alex was her dream. She looked over at the man she was about to marry and debated whether to share her concerns, ultimately deciding against it.

They're unfounded worries. Nothing concrete. No need to 'borrow trouble," as Granny would say.

"Hey, Monie."

"Yeah."

"The MMC tree lighting and food truck festival is on Friday."

She checked her phone's calendar. "You're right. You wanna go?"

"Yeah, and we could take that picture that we skipped last year." He glanced at her with a sly smile.

"At the mistletoe booth?"

"We can commemorate our second first kiss."

Monique chuckled and shook her head. *He's a mess, but I love him.*

"Sounds good, Alexander. It's a date."

Chapter 7: Both
For Better, For Worse

Friday, December 13 — 8 days until the wedding

Monique sat next to Alex on the loveseat in the Grace Life Church counseling room for their last session with Pastor Reginald, forcing herself not to think about the day's date. Friday the 13th.

I don't believe in superstitions. Why is it on my mind today?

"Today our topic is For Better, For Worse. That means if right now is as good as it gets and it's only downhill from here, you still stay. Now, that doesn't mean that you take abuse or mistreatment. God isn't abusive, demeaning, belittling, dismissive, manipulative, or inconsiderate. So, we shouldn't be that way to each other."

Pastor Reginald waited for them to acknowledge their agreement with him before he continued.

"'For better' is the easy part. We love the better, the health, the richer. But 'for worse' challenges us because it means you have to work through conflict. Don't believe anyone who tells you they've never had conflict in their marriage. Disagreements are inevitable. Because there's no one on the planet that you agree with one hundred percent of the time. Not even yourself."

Monique sat up. "What do you mean?"

"Have you done or said some things that at the time you thought were okay, but later realized they weren't?"

Both she and Alex nodded.

"Exactly. So today, we're discussing how to work through the conflicts that come up in a relationship."

Conflict resolution was also a topic in their Atlanta premarital counseling class. But considering their five previous sessions, Monique figured the more tools they had, the better.

"What is your communication style? How do you handle disagreements? Do you pray to get direction from God first, or do you jump right in, thinking you know how to handle it?"

Ouch.

"I say that because that's how I used to approach disagreements with my wife early in our marriage." He chuckled and shook his head. "But my wife helped me to see the error of my ways."

Alex smiled. "Knowing Sister Salekia, I'm sure she did."

"Yep. Which brings us to today's activity. Pick a topic from your sessions with Pastors Mike and Olivia that you have differing opinions on."

"I have one," Alex quickly said.

Monique pressed her lips together and looked straight ahead.

"Okay, Alex. What is it?"

"Balancing family," he motioned between himself and Monique, "and work."

She didn't blink under Pastor Reginald's assessing gaze, but she rolled her eyes internally.

How many times are we going to talk about this?

"Okay, sounds like this is a continuing discussion. So, Alex, you take Monique's perspective, and Monique, you take his."

"What?" they said at the same time.

"Switching roles helps each of you see the conflict from the other's point of view. You can hear their heart. It helps foster empathy and understanding."

I understand that this could go sideways.

"Monique, start with what you hear to be Alex's concern." He leaned back on the loveseat and put his ankle on the opposite knee.

She took a deep breath, then cleared her throat.

"Work shouldn't come before family. If you're working late every night, you're not giving our relationship what it deserves." She tried to maintain a neutral tone, despite being irritated.

Alex bristled.

Guess I didn't quite get there.

"My work matters. I've worked hard to succeed. And I have to work even harder to stay on top. If you can't handle that... well, maybe it's more your problem than mine," he responded harshly.

Pastor Reginald sat up. "Remember, you're practicing empathy, not scoring points," he said, trying to mediate.

"Well, maybe if someone stopped making me sound unreasonable, I'd feel like this was empathy," Monique said.

"Same," Alex replied.

"Both of you take a breath," Pastor Reginald ordered.

They did as they were told.

"Okay, let's try this again. Monique, go ahead."

"Work is just work, Monie, and it'll always be there." She looked Alex in the eye and lifted one shoulder. "So what if you miss a deadline or lose a client? It isn't more important than family time. Your business will be fine."

She again tried to keep the edge out of her voice, but seeing that Alex narrowed his eyes and pressed his lips into a thin line, she probably failed to. Again. Monique raised her eyebrows and hoped he could read her thoughts.

You're the one who suggested this topic.

"Empower PR is more than work, Alex. My business is who I am. If you love me, you'll accept that my business comes before you." His words were sharp and clipped.

Monique opened her mouth to respond, but Pastor Reginald spoke first.

"Careful. You're supposed to be speaking *for* each other, not *at* each other."

She was over it and didn't even attempt to hide the sarcasm.

"It should be obvious to you to spend less time building your business so you don't neglect your husband. Because what's several years of hard work and amazing accomplishments compared to being at home barefoot and in the kitchen every night by six o'clock?"

"My job is my passion. If you loved me, you'd understand that. And if I want to work until midnight chasing success, you should deal with it."

She stiffened at his clipped delivery and accusing tone.

"Remember, this isn't about winning. It's about seeing the issue from the other's POV."

Pastor Reginald attempted to redirect them once again, but the mood in the room had shifted.

Monique shot to her feet. "Empower PR Partners is not just a job or a business, Alex. I've explained our mission and purpose to you several times. And shared how and why its launch was delayed. By years. How do you not know this?"

Alex stood and faced her. "Monie, I know Empower is important, but it's not the most important thing in your life. There are some things that come before it. Right?"

"Of course there are. But that doesn't mean Empower never takes priority. It's situation-dependent." She pressed her hand to her forehead.

How does he not get this? How does he not get me?

"It seems like every situation is in Empower's favor." He shook his head and huffed.

Is he jealous of Empower PR?

"That's because I don't shout it from the rooftop and wear it like a badge of honor when I choose us over work."

His eyebrows shot up. "Are you saying that I do?"

"Yes." Her arms shot out to the sides. "Every time I have to work, you list all the times you could have stayed late, but instead you came to spend time with me. As if I'm supposed to be so grateful that King Alex came down from his big, important throne to spend time with the lowly peasant girl selling apples at the market."

"Okay, stop," Pastor Reginald commanded. "You two aren't role-playing anymore. You're fighting. That's not the exercise."

Monique turned away from Alex and folded her arms. She couldn't see his face, but anger rolled off of him in tangible waves.

Good.

"This exercise was supposed to open your eyes, not wound each other. What I'm hearing are fears—real ones—that need to be faced with honesty, not defensiveness." His tone was gentler but still firm.

"You're both very passionate about your perspectives. But from what I've seen, the past three sessions, you're also passionate about each other. You need to come to an agreement where you both give and receive. Marriage isn't about avoiding conflict. It's about how you handle it when it comes."

Neither of them responded. Monique was still fuming, so while she heard Pastor Reginald's words, they didn't penetrate.

He sighed. "This is not how I would have liked our last session to end, but it's real life. Some conversations will continue for years because they are big issues that don't have a quick fix."

Pastor Reginald stood and waited for them to face him before he continued.

"This isn't insurmountable. However, you have to be willing to genuinely listen to each other. Not just wait for the other person to finish talking so you can speak. Instead, hear the heart behind their words."

He placed one hand on Monique's shoulder and the other on Alex's. "Let's pray."

As Monique and Alex walked tight-lipped to their vehicles, she reflected on Pastor Reginald's words at the beginning of the session.

If today is as good as it gets, we're in trouble.

***

Monique was glad she and Alex had driven separately so they could each run errands after their session. They needed space.

"I'm, uh, going to pick up my tux," Alex said from ten feet away without looking at her.

"Yeah. I'm going to pick up my dress."

Even though I might not need it.

"Ok. I'll… I'll text you." He got in his car and drove off.

What more did she expect? That he was going to say he didn't mean anything he said during the session? That he finally understood her point of view? Even if he had said that, he wouldn't have truly meant it. Just as she wouldn't have truly meant it if she'd said it to him.

She sighed and got into her SUV. They were at an impasse.

The first few bars of Here Comes the Bride came from her phone. She barked out a humorless laugh. Using that song as a reminder to pick up her wedding dress seemed like a good idea at the time she set it. But in that moment, it was mocking her.

Although her wedding hung in the balance, she had an appointment to get to. She pushed the button to start her SUV.

Don't want to pay storage fees for the dress on top of having another failed engagement.

***

Monique parked next to Stacey's car when she arrived at The Dress Shoppe. Her mother's car, along with Mom Imogene's, Auntie Thelma's, and Auntie Anne's, were also in the lot.

I guess I'm the last to arrive.

A soft chime sounded as she walked through the door, then laughter floated from the back of the store.

I recognize those voices.

She nodded at the receptionist, then went to join her party. They were all smiling, chatting, and sipping beverages. Clearly, her presence wasn't needed to get the party started.

"Should I ask what's in those glasses?"

"Monique!" "Sweetheart!" "Mo!" They all rushed forward to hug her.

Hugging Alex's mom and aunt felt awkward. She forced a smile while they gushed over how great she looked and how happy they were for her and Alex.

If only they knew.

"Darla, she's here," her mother called to the bridal consultant.

Darla materialized. "Your dress is in the fitting room. Are you ready?"

Monique must have hesitated a beat too long.

"Sweetheart," her mother put her hand on Monique's shoulder and studied her face, "are you okay? Is everything alright?" Her brow furrowed.

All the other ladies stopped talking and focused on her.

Great.

"Yes, yes. I'm fine," she lied. "Just a little tired. You know, lots to do."

Everyone nodded and voiced their agreement and understanding.

"When was the last time you ate something?" her Aunt Thelma asked.

Monique shook her head. "Not since breakfast."

A chorus of "Ah, that explains it," followed.

"Try on your dress, then we can go get lunch," her mother directed.

"Follow me," Darla said, "and I'll get you in and out in no time."

Monique grabbed Stacey's arm. "Actually, if you don't mind, Darla, my maid of honor had her heart set on helping."

"I did?" Stacey whispered to her.

Monique squeezed Stacey's elbow.

"Yes, we've dreamed of this day since we were young girls having tea parties in our princess dresses," Stacey said.

Monique cut her eyes at Stacey. *She's overdoing it, but if it works, I won't argue.*

"Well, okay," Darla reluctantly agreed, "but don't hesitate to call out if you get stuck. You don't want to damage the dress. At this late date, it may not be able to be repaired in time for the wedding."

"We'll be extra careful and will ask for help if needed," Monique assured her.

Darla walked Stacey and Monique back to the dressing room, then joined the other ladies.

"Okay, spill," Stacey said.

Monique sighed and dropped onto the tufted bench.

"It's over, Stace."

"What's over?"

"Me and Alex."

She gave Stacey a detailed overview of the morning's counseling session. Anger and irritation boiled in her belly as she repeated the things Alex had said. But her voice caught in her throat when she described the distance in his eyes when they parted.

Monique closed her eyes to keep tears from falling. "I don't see how we can get past it. We're too far apart for a meeting in the middle to be acceptable for either of us."

Stacey shook her head. "I don't believe that, Mo. I think Alex just needs reassurance of his place in your life. What did your dad say?"

"A man wants to know that he has the heart of the woman who has his."

Stacey shrugged. "There you go. Show him that in a way that resonates with him."

Monique dropped her head back and looked up at the ceiling. "You make it sound so easy."

"Oh, that was not my intent at all. It won't be easy, but that doesn't mean it's impossible either."

"You two doing alright back there?" Darla called out.

"Yes!" they answered in unison.

Stacey unzipped the dress bag and stalled. "Um, you might want to get Darla back here. I have no idea where to start."

Monique laughed. "Good idea."

Darla didn't blink an eye at Monique still being completely dressed in street clothes. Monique figured that she and Stacey were probably not the first bride and maid of honor to need a moment alone. While

Darla helped Monique into the dress, she showed Stacey all the tricks for getting it on and off snag-free.

As expected, all the ladies oohed and aahed over Monique in the dress. Her mother even teared up. After several turns in the trifold mirror and seeing herself at every possible angle, Monique was finally out of her wedding dress and alone in the dressing room.

She was contemplating her situation when she received a text from Alex.

Alexander Patterson: Tree lighting tonight?

Monique was still miffed, but if they were going to make it, she had to meet him at least halfway. She didn't want to give up too quickly.

Monique: Sure.

***

Alex put his phone away and stepped out of the truck. Instead of heading straight to the formalwear shop after leaving Grace Life Church, he drove around to clear his mind. But it had the opposite effect, as he found himself in places linked to his relationship with Monique. The Christmas Store, Dee's Kitchen, The Peabody, Emerald Thai, the arcade. He even drove past the midway where he'd won Henry the dolphin for her.

Could all those times have meant nothing? Or less

than he thought? How could he have gone from feeling like they were meant to be together to being unsure of their future?

He got out of the truck and was met at the entrance to the formalwear shop by Marquis's smirking face.

"Monique?"

Marquis had apparently seen him send the text and wait for the response.

Yeah, but not in the way you think.

"Um, yeah. We're going to the tree lighting."

"Ah, yes. Where it all began." He opened the door and held it open for Alex to follow. "Well, that's not entirely true. It all began in middle high school."

"And it might all be ending now."

Marquis spun around to face him. "What?"

"She loves her business more than me."

He blew a raspberry. "Dude, you're crazy."

"Am I?" The more he thought about it, the clearer it became. "I had to take the job in Atlanta because she wouldn't move her business to Memphis."

"Wasn't she on her way back to Memphis to tell you she was willing to do dual residence or even long distance to be with you?"

Okay, there may be a slight flaw in my logic, but it's mostly true.

The tailor nodded at Alex and pointed him to the dressing room.

He stepped into the tuxedo pants. The material was smooth and cool against his skin. He pulled on the crisp, white dress shirt and fingered the French cuffs. His father's antique silver cufflinks came to mind.

I might not get to wear them after all.

He adjusted the turndown collar. After deciding to skip the tie, he shrugged into the jacket and looked at himself in the mirror.

Not bad, Alexander.

His stomach clenched at Monique's pet name for him. Only she was allowed to call him that.

Monique's reply was only one word, but she agreed to a date. At the place where they began their more-than-just-friends relationship. That had to mean something.

Maybe all we need is a break from counseling and wedding preparations. A walk by the river in the glow of the light show on the bridge could be just the thing to get them back to Monie Love and Alexander Patterson.

***

Alex and Monique huddled together to ward off the cold and joined in the countdown for the tree lighting.

"…five, four, three, two, one!"

The twenty-five-foot tree lit up. Blinking white lights wound their way around red and green ornaments of varying sizes and shapes.

"It's different from last year," Monique said over the claps, cheers, and whistles.

Did she mean them or the tree?

"What?"

"Last year, the lights and ornaments were multicolored. It's nice that they changed it up."

"Yeah, it is." A thought came to him. "Unlike the display at the Christmas Store."

Monique burst out in laughter just as Alex had intended. Their aunts had insisted the window display be exactly as it was when Alex and Monique were kids.

They reached a tentative truce as they perused the food trucks and had a pleasant conversation over dinner. Neither brought up the counseling session nor their argument. But it hung between them. It wasn't the usual comfortable, at-home feel he had whenever they were together, but he prayed that they were on their way back.

Alex was further encouraged when Monique took his hand as they retraced their steps past the food trucks and the tree, on the way to the path in Thorpe Park along the river.

He broke the silence.

"We're decorating the tree after church on Sunday, then having a family dinner. You're joining us again this year, right?"

Monique stopped in her tracks and turned to face him. "I'm going with my family to *Handel's Messiah* on Sunday night."

Oh no.

Attending *Messiah* wasn't part of his normal activities. He'd completely forgotten about it. But he remembered their discussion.

"I thought we said we'd incorporate both of them."

She disengaged her hand from his, and a part of him went with it.

"Then why didn't you mention going to the Messiah? Do your parents know we'd have to leave early? Or are they starting earlier so we can be at both the whole time?"

Rubbed the back of his neck, then focused on the wreath-making stand behind her. Decorating the house and then having a family dinner were two of the things he looked forward to most every year. His mother had been planning and talking about it for weeks and was preparing his favorite dishes. He didn't want to leave early and disappoint her. Or himself. It would feel wrong.

"Maybe we could start attending both next year."

She tilted her head. "Oh. Then, since we did your family event last year, we'll do mine this year. Right?"

He struggled to find a diplomatic way to tell her that he had no desire to see the Messiah. An interactive family event fostered stronger relationships than attending a concert. But he must have remained silent too long.

Monique threw up her hand. The universal symbol for "stop." "Don't worry about it. You do the tree and dinner with your family, and I'll do the Messiah with mine."

"Monie, I—"

"I said, don't worry about it."

She spun on her heels and resumed walking. He fell

in step beside her. A cool breeze washed over them—literally and figuratively. As they walked in uncomfortable silence, Alex partly wished he hadn't brought the subject up. However, a larger part insisted that exposing the flaws in their relationship was necessary for them to make the right decision for their future. As undesirable as it may have felt.

"Come take a picture with your sweetheart under the mistletoe," the proprietor of the booth called out as they passed by.

The photographer unknowingly mocked Alex. One of his main reasons for returning to the tree lighting was to take the picture that he and Monique hadn't taken the year before. Considering she walked with her arms folded across her chest and looking straight ahead, taking a cute couple pic was probably the furthest thing from her mind.

But nothing ventured, nothing gained.

Alex touched Monique's arm to stop her, raised his eyebrow, and gestured with his head at the mistletoe booth. She looked over then back at him. After a beat, she shrugged and wordlessly headed over to the booth. He followed.

They stood under the mistletoe, just looking at each other for a moment. Alex searched her eyes, hoping to discern her thoughts, but he came up empty. He reached for her waist. She stepped into his arms and put her hands on his shoulders. Alex bent his head, and she touched her lips to his. As soon as the camera clicked, she stepped away.

Technically, they had taken a picture kissing under the mistletoe. But it didn't feel like their kiss the year before. It was distant. Maybe even obligatory.

So much for reliving a romantic moment.

Alex acknowledged the possibility that they were on the brink of breaking up a week before the wedding.

This isn't better. And I pray it doesn't get worse.

Chapter 8: Monique
For Richer, For Poorer

Saturday, December 14 — 7 days until the wedding

Monique pulled into the parking lot of First Christian Church to attend the first counseling session with Pastor Cynthia, her childhood co-pastor. To her surprise, Alex was already there. She parked next to his truck, her truck, their truck. Was it their truck anymore? With the heated disagreements and distance between them, she wasn't sure.

Could they come this far to quit? If they did, then what? There was definitely no way to go back to being friends this time. Was she forging ahead because she couldn't see another way? After debating into the wee hours of the morning whether to cancel their session, she decided to see it through to the end. Not going to counseling wouldn't help it.

Hopefully, going won't hurt it even more.

She got out and shivered at the drastic change from the warmth of her SUV to the brisk wind outside. The temperature had gotten colder over the past few days, the weather mimicking their relationship. She hoped the trend would continue, since a warming was predicted over the weekend.

Monique and Alex greeted one another with

awkward cordiality, a side hug followed by a peck on the cheek. It was drastically different from what felt like a month prior, but had only been a week, when they started the pre-marital counseling sessions. But then they were drastically different.

So much has happened and come to light.

She held in a sigh as they silently walked side by side into the church.

***

Monique and Alex stood in the outer office while the assistant announced their arrival.

"Pastor Cynthia," she spoke softly into the receiver, "Monique Lovelace and Alex Patterson are here." She nodded and looked up at them as she hung up. "You can go on back. She's ready for you."

They walked down the short hallway and were greeted by Pastor Cynthia at the door. She was impeccably dressed and had a warm, friendly smile, as always.

"Monique," she embraced her, "It's good to see you. And Alex," she clasped his hand in both of hers, "you as well. Please, please, come in and sit down." She motioned to the sitting area.

Monique and Alex took the two chairs, leaving the two-cushion sofa for Pastor Cynthia. She stumbled slightly as she changed course and sat on the sofa.

She studied their faces for a moment. "So, how has the counseling been thus far?"

Monique was sure Pastors Mike and Reginald had shared overviews of their sessions with them, if not full details. So, she went with the same answer she'd given to Pastor Reginald.

"Challenging."

It was true, but had a different meaning than when she first said it. Alex nodded in agreement.

"I see. Well, that is the intent of these sessions. To get couples to look beneath the surface to the root of issues. Some of them, you'll spend a lifetime working through."

Or not.

Neither Monique nor Alex responded.

"You two are awfully quiet this morning. Is everything okay?"

Monique wanted to scream that nothing was okay, but she couldn't bring herself to admit it aloud. So, she dropped her gaze to her hands and wondered whether she should cancel her manicure appointment.

"It's been a really long week. We've had our scheduled wedding responsibilities, some unexpected wedding issues, and the counseling sessions with homework. We're both really…tired," Alex said diplomatically.

Pastor Cynthia nodded, but her expression indicated she knew more than fatigue was to blame. "Well then, let's get started. Hopefully, you can get some rest over the weekend since you don't have a session on Sunday."

Please don't ask what we're doing on Sunday.

Pastor Cynthia either didn't see Alex stiffen or she chose to ignore it.

"We're continuing with the vows. So today is For Richer, For Poorer. While finances are the obvious topic, several aspects should be discussed and agreed upon."

She handed them a sheet of paper to share. When they leaned toward each other to read it, Monique noticed that Pastor Cynthia had two more copies of it on the small table in front of the sofa.

Monique made contact with Pastor Cynthia's sharp and assessing eyes. Then she slightly raised one eyebrow, daring Monique to question her actions. Monique shifted her focus back to the paper she'd been given.

This round goes to you, Pastor.

Pastor Cynthia crossed her ankles and started the discussion.

"As Christians, we say that we trust God with our finances, but that can mean different things to each person. What does that mean to you, and what does it mean to your future spouse?"

Alex looked at Monique and nodded. They had answered that question during the class at their Atlanta church, so they were already in agreement on that one. At least.

Pastor Cynthia continued. "How much and how often do you give? What organizations or causes do you support? Do you give or loan money to people? I'm sure you've had a family member or friend ask to borrow money at some point."

They both nodded.

Don't even get me started.

"You need to be on the same page, so that people outside of your union don't cause tension within it."

We're causing enough tension on our own, thank you.

"How will you set up your household finances? Will you have separate accounts that both of you have access to, or will you put everything in one account? Does Alex get access to the business account? Does Monique get access to the properties' accounts?"

Monique's head was swimming, and they hadn't even gotten through half of the list.

Pastor Cynthia put her paper on top of the one already on the table.

"I won't read through the rest of the list. However, if there are topics that you haven't already discussed, I strongly suggest addressing them *before* the wedding. Money issues are one of the most common reasons for divorce."

Alex let go of the piece of paper that connected them. Monique folded it and slid it into her tablet cover.

"In today's session, we'll focus on spending and saving priorities. Please understand, my goal isn't to tell you how to structure your financial life. There are several ways to do it. No one way works for every couple. The two of you determine the best way for you."

Pastor Cynthia handed them a worksheet with three columns: Spend, Save, and Give.

"I want each of you to list your top two or three priorities in each column."

Monique hazarded a glance at Alex at the same time he looked at her. He lifted his eyebrows and shoulders slightly, then started writing. After they put their pens down and looked up, Pastor Cynthia spoke.

"Monique, please share your list."

Here we go.

"I think it's important that we set aside money to spend on travel, experiences, and a few luxuries. We should save for reinvestment in our businesses and future family expenses. And of course, give to our church and charitable causes."

Pastor Cynthia kept a neutral expression. "Alex?"

"I think our spending should focus on home improvements and our future kids' education. We save for additional investment properties, retirement, and an emergency fund. And give to our church and set up a long-term charitable trust."

"It's good that you both give and value saving, but there are some differences in what you have prioritized for spending and saving. Who'd like to go first?"

Alex shifted in his chair to face Monique. She reminded herself to keep an open mind.

"I'm not against traveling, experiences, or a few luxuries, but if we have to choose, home improvement and education should take priority."

"I agree that those would be priorities once we have

purchased a home and have children," she measured her words, "but what about now? We agreed we'd live in my townhome until we need more space. You won't be paying rent anymore, so that will free up some money. And we don't have kids, yet."

And may not be able to.

"That's true," Alex admitted.

Monique released a sigh. Maybe they were going to get through a session without—

"But…"

I celebrated too soon.

"I just think if we buckle down for a few years, we can afford more luxuries later. You could even stop working."

She couldn't hold it tougher any longer.

"Why do you hate the idea of my working?" She didn't care if she was slightly off topic. They needed to get to the bottom of this.

He stiffened, then glanced at Pastor Cynthia before turning back to Monique. "I didn't say that. I said I could get to a place where you don't have to work. Then you'd have choices."

She dropped her forehead into her hands. *This cannot be happening.*

"My choice, Alex, is to continue to grow Empower PR Partners. My business isn't just a paycheck. It's my dream. I'm proud of what I've built, and I'm excited about its future. I've made that clear in practically every session that we've had. But you continue to belittle it as if it's a temp job to pay off a credit card bill."

Alex's jaw clenched and unclenched before he responded. "I'm not saying close it down, but it doesn't have to be everything. If we're financially secure, you won't have to stress yourself over deadlines or clients."

"I've built—"

"You keep talking about the life you've built," he interrupted with a hint of irritation in his voice. "You're not the only one who has established themselves, Monie. I have, too." He stood, then sighed. "But I'm not clinging to it like you are."

Heat rose in her neck. She slowly rose to her feet. "You don't have to defend your life because I'm not asking you to sacrifice it."

"I don't –"

"Yes, you do." Her body trembled with anger. "And you have a double standard."

His arms shot out to his sides. "How?"

"You have a problem when I work late or have to take a call after hours, but when you do it's fine."

"Because I'm securing our future," he said as he sat down.

"And what am I doing, playing dress-up?" She sat and faced him. "If it's *our* future, shouldn't *I* be allowed to contribute? What if Empower PR becomes big enough that *you* don't have to work? You could bring your operational and organizational skills to Empower and concentrate on your investment properties."

He squirmed in his seat.

"Oh, you don't like that, huh? It's okay for me to scale back on my dream, but not you."

"I never said that." Alex shook his head.

Monique scoffed. "You just did."

"Enough," Pastor Cynthia raised her hand before they could go further. "You've strayed from the topic. The exercise wasn't about proving who's right with money or whose job is more important. It was about learning what your priorities reveal about your hearts. Right now, I hear wounds speaking louder than love."

Monique turned away from Alex, crossed her arms, and blinked back tears of frustration. As hard as she had tried to prevent it, it was happening again. She would have to choose between her relationship and her dream. She felt Alex's eyes boring into her back, but she refused to flinch.

Pastor Cynthia leaned forward and spoke in a firm tone.

"Alex, Monique's business is tied to her sense of self and her life's purpose. When you dismiss it, she feels like you're dismissing her. Monique, Alex's financial plans are tied to his desire to provide for and protect his family. When you reject them, it says that you want or trust him. Until you can listen to each other and address these issues, every disagreement will feel like a battle you have to win. And marriage does not survive when winning matters more than understanding."

Pastor Cynthia stood. "We'll stop here for today. Go

home, pray, and think on what you heard in your own heart—not just what you said aloud."

They walked out to the parking lot in silence. Alex waited for Monique to get in her SUV, then waved goodbye. Monique drove away, more convinced than ever that Alex just didn't understand.

How could she marry someone who didn't get her?

***

Monique listened while Stacey and Tara alternated between singing along with the radio and giving life updates. It was a much-needed distraction from her relationship drama. And it allowed her to pretend that she and Alex might actually make it to the altar the following Saturday. Although the chance of that was looking slimmer by the minute.

Tara turned around in the passenger's seat and faced Monique. "I'm glad you got to come to the Merry Memphis Christmas BBQ + Blues tonight. I know the wedding party dinner was just on Wednesday, but it feels like it's been much longer since I've seen you."

Had it only been three days since she was cuddled up with Alex, reveling in how well the day had gone? It didn't seem real, considering they'd barely said two words to each other since they left the counseling session that morning.

"It does feel like that was at least a week ago," Monique agreed.

"Hey," Tara said, "this might be your last Girls'

Night as a single woman. We have to do it up!" She turned the music up and started dancing in her seat.

Maybe not.

At the light, Stacey caught Monique's eyes in the rearview mirror, but Monique quickly looked away. She didn't want to give even a hint as to how bad things were between her and Alex, not until…

Until when, exactly?

Monique couldn't shake the feeling that Alex would be happier if she completely closed Empower PR down and played house. She meant no disrespect to anyone who wanted to. It just wasn't what *she* wanted. But with each session, she became more convinced that it was what Alex wanted.

Can I give him that? Will he resent me if I don't? Will I resent him if I do?

After Stacey parked, the trio got out of the car and followed their noses and ears. The smell of hickory and mesquite smoke led them to the pitmasters and thus the food. The sounds of classic blues songs drew them to the stage.

"I know we're stopping by Raineshaven," Stacey said, pointing to Monique.

"Gotta check on my client. And the food is ah-may-zing."

"Agreed. Any other places definitely on the list? Or do we just want to walk around and see what looks good?" Stacey asked.

"Interstate is on my definite list, but I'm good with walking around. We'll eventually come across it."

Monique's text message chime sounded. Actually, it was the text message chime specifically assigned to Alex.

"I bet I know who that is," Tara said, bumping Monique's shoulder.

She managed a half-smile and checked her phone.

> **Alexander Patterson:** Hey. Have a good time with the girls tonight. Marq and I are hanging.

She sent back an equally dull message.

> **Monique:** Thanks. You, too. Tell Marquis I said hi.

Just as she dropped her phone in her handbag, Merry Christmas Baby poured through the speakers and transported her back a year. She felt Alex's arms around her, smelled his woodsy cologne, and heard their hearts beating the same rhythm.

Tears sprang to her eyes. Then she vigorously shook her head.

No.

She wasn't going to think about how far they were from that couple until she absolutely had to. She would eat some good food, listen to some good music, and have a good time with her friends. And delude herself into thinking her life wasn't about to crash down around her.

*****

Monique took the back seat again for the ride from BBQ and Blues back to Stacy's house. However, she was more engaged than she had been on her way to the event. Good food, good music, and time with two of her best friends had chased away the blues. Even if only temporarily. She laughed, sang, and told stories along with them.

When Stacey pulled into her driveway, Monique still hadn't decided whether to stay the night at Stacey's or go back to RJ and Yvette's house. She packed an overnight bag, claiming she might be too tired to drive home or that she didn't want to disturb them if it was really late. While both of those were considerations, the real reason was that she didn't want to answer questions about Alex. More specifically,
Alex's absence over the past few days.

"Why do we have so much food? Who's going to eat all this?" Monique asked while they got out of the car.

Tara bought enough rib tips and smoked sausages from Interstate to feed her family for a week. Stacey loaded up on chicken, pulled pork, and brisket from Mary's Pit BBQ as if they were closing for good. And like last year, Raineshaven loaded her up with four Styrofoam containers, filled to the brim.

"You can freeze barbecue, you know," Stacey replied.

"That's true." Monique handed one of the covered aluminum foil pans to Tara. "Make sure you hold it under the bottom, it's heavy. Stacey, you take this bag," she extended the bag that held the plasticware, extra sauce, and wet-naps, "so you can open the door."

Stacey waved her off. "No, you take that and go open the door," she pressed her key ring into Monique's hand. "Tara and I will bring the food in."

Stacey's directions struck her as strange, but she didn't argue. She'd had enough arguing for a year. "Okay."

Monique chuckled softly as she headed up the walkway, followed by Stacey and Tara. The cool December night brushed her cheeks. Her flats lightly thumped against the concrete, and the lingering scent of barbecue clung to her jacket.

"I'm just saying, if that band had played 'Gravity,' I might've torn that stage up, like the Harp on *The Masked Singer*."

Tara adjusted her load of takeout containers. "The man at the next table was listening like he wanted to give you a record deal. Among other things."

Monique snorted. "He was looking at my plate, not me. I had the last rib."

The motion sensor light came on before her foot hit the doorstep.

She unlocked the door and stepped inside the dark, quiet house. Nothing seemed out of place, but it felt…different. She cautiously flipped on the light in the foyer.

"Surprise!" echoed through the house.

Monique jumped and clutched her chest. Then she stood in a daze while her brain caught up with what she was seeing. Streamers hung from the ceiling, gold and white balloons bobbed above a table covered with cupcakes and punch. Desiree waved a noisemaker. Aniya held a phone high, recording. Even the Christmas tree glowed a little brighter, as if it were in on the plan.

"Oh, wow!"

She bent at the waist and covered her open mouth with her hands. Tears of joy sprang to her eyes. It felt good to have a happy cry for a change.

She pulled Desiree and Aniya into a hug and rocked back and forth. "When did you get in? How did you set all this up?" She released them and turned to Stacey and Tara. "You two were in on this the whole time?" They nodded. "I can't believe you keep it a secret." A lightbulb went off in her head. "Now, I know why there's so much extra food."

"Yep," Desiree said, then bit into a rib. "We were willing to miss the blues, but not the barbecue."

Monique moved further into the house to the great room. "But you guys already gave me a bridal shower two months ago."

"Yeah, but this one is just for The Crew," Aniya said.

"You know we like our exclusive, private events," Tara added.

"That's true," Monique agreed.

"And since you will most likely be otherwise occupied when we regularly meet..." Desiree shimmied her shoulders.

Monique shook her head. "No comment."

"Oh, you don't have to comment. We already

know," Stacey called from the kitchen.

"You needed one last Crew hangout as a single woman," Desiree finished.

Monique's smile faltered a bit, but she caught it before anyone noticed. Or at least commented about it.

"Then let's get it started."

Monique let Aniya slip a glittery sash over her shoulder and place a plastic tiara topped with a sparkly *Bride to Be* sign on her head.

Just keep smiling. They mean well. Nobody needs to know what happened this morning.

"And," Stacey said, "I found a CD by DJ Lawbreaker with all the 90s and early 2000s hip-hop and R&B hits." She pushed play, and the room filled with all of their jams from back in the day.

They talked and ate. Well, Desiree and Aniya ate. Monique, Stacey, and Tara were still full. Monique laughed and played along, while internally she was preoccupied with how fragile things felt with Alex. Even the decorations—white poinsettias, twinkle lights, "Bride to Be" garland—felt almost mocking to her unease. Still, she was determined not to ruin the night. So, when Desiree announced it was time to play games, she responded enthusiastically.

"This is What Did the Groom Say? with a twist. Instead of asking Alex questions about you, we asked questions about him. We," Desiree pointed to herself, Stacey, and Tara, "have each guessed how many questions you will get right. Each of Alex's answers is sealed in its own envelope, so no one could peek at them ahead of time."

Huh. I can't believe Alex managed to keep that secret from me. He usually can't hold water.

"How did you get the answers from Alex?"

"Oh, we had Marquis get them. We told him it was to put together a surprise gift. So, he just brought up in conversation any questions he didn't know the answer to. Alex was none the wiser."

Monique chuckled. *That explains it.*

"Let's see how you do, Mo. No pressure, but I'm counting on you. There are some really good prizes over there." Desiree said. "I know because I picked them out."

Monique easily rattled off his favorite food, movie, TV show, and candy. His biggest pet peeve and the dish he loves for her to cook were no-brainers.

"Okay, Miss Perfect Score, when was your first kiss?"

She hesitated. Their actual first kiss was at the eighth-grade dance. But they vowed never to speak of it, and they hadn't. Until the year before, at the MMC tree lighting. Where they had their real first kiss. Technically, it was their second kiss. But it was their first acknowledged kiss.

"Wait, you don't know when your first kiss was?" Aniya asked.

"Of course, I do. It's just that…"

"What? You can only have one first kiss." Tara said.

"Not necessarily," she drew out.

Stacey put her cup down. "Spill."

"So, we kinda kissed the night of our eighth-grade dance." She closed her eyes and winced, preparing for the onslaught.

"I knew it!"

"What? No way!"

"How are we just finding this out?"

"So much for being 'just friends.'"

"Wait, didn't you go to the dance with Carlos Mason?"

They all spoke at once, and since Monique's eyes were closed, she wasn't sure who said what.

She waved her hands and shook her head. "No, no, no. It wasn't like that."

"Then explain what it *was* like," Aniya said.

Monique massaged her forehead, then looked at her friends with a sigh.

"We'd both gone outside to get some air and ran into each other."

"You ran into each other's lips?" Desiree asked.

She sighed and rolled her eyes. "Can I finish?"

Desiree motioned for her to continue.

"We sat down on that bench behind the gym."

"The make-out bench?" Tara asked.

She looked up in frustration at the ceiling. "Do you want me to tell the story or not?"

"Proceed," Tara said, not trying to hide her smile in the least.

"Thank you. We talked about middle school, high

school, and the DJ. The next thing I knew, he kissed me."

"Did you kiss him back?" Stacey tucked her lips in, her body shaking with silent laughter.

She dropped her head. *I can't lie to them. They're my best friends and bridesmaids.*

"Yes," she admitted softly.

The room erupted in whoops and hollers. Aniya jumped up. Stacey ran to the kitchen and back. Tara lay out on the floor, with her arms out to the side. And Desiree spun around in a circle. One would have thought they were at a church revival.

"Oh, calm down! It lasted a few seconds –"

"Like, one Mississippi… two Mississippi…?" Stacey asked, drawing out her words.

"Yeah, exactly how many is 'a few,'" Desiree asked using air quotes.

Monique turned her head away from them and shrugged. "I don't know."

"Yes, you do," Tara insisted.

"It was twenty-five years ago."

"Uh-huh. You still know." Tara wasn't backing off.

"Not exactly."

"Ballpark it," Aniya demanded.

Monique's face flushed, and her entire body broke out in a sweat. Because even though she and Alex hadn't spoken about that day until the year before, she remembered it. Vividly.

"Um… ten or fifteen?"

"Well, alright, Alex," Desiree said.

"Anyway," Monique waved her hands wildly, "we kissed and promised to never mention it. And we didn't until last year at the tree lighting. When we kissed for real." She prayed The Crew would move on to the next question.

"Uh, ma'am. Fifteen seconds? That *is* a real kiss," Tara said.

I knew better before I prayed.

"Fine. Can we get back to the game? What did Alex say?" Monique asked.

Desiree ripped open the envelope. "We had two—at the eighth-grade dance and the tree lighting last year." She blinked rapidly. "Wow. You and Alex are frighteningly on the same page."

We used to be.

Or were they ever? Sure, all the answers to the game rolled off her tongue. But the past week had taught her that knowing facts about him and knowing his mind and heart were vastly different. Had he been showing her what he thought she wanted to see? Had she been doing the same?

"I'm… I'm not sure about that anymore," she admitted.

Stacey frowned. "What do you mean, Mo?"

The room grew quiet and serious.

"It's been a lot, y'all." She fought back tears.

Is breaking down in front of them going to become a Christmas tradition?

Desiree sat next to her on the sofa. "What has been a lot?"

She blew out a breath. "These counseling sessions. We went through counseling in Atlanta and touched on some of the same topics. However, it was a larger class, and we only had three one-on-one sessions. There were no activities or homework. But this," she searched for the words, "this is more intense. And personal. And…"

Frightening, scary, and concerning all came to mind, but she couldn't bring herself to say either of those words.

"Real?" Tara asked.

Monique nodded.

"Yeah, I remember that feeling." Tara sat on the floor in front of the sofa. "Nick and I almost quit because the sessions were so intense." She shrugged. "But we didn't, and we made it through. I'll be honest, there were times when I didn't think we would. But then I thought about the thousands of couples who had made it through. And if they could do it, so could we. The key is deciding to do what's hard to get to where you want to be."

Desiree nodded. "Thinking that everything will be easy with the 'right' person is a fallacy. You're going to have conflict, but you can work through it if you choose to."

"Yeah, all the pastors have said that in some form or another."

"And, of course, there's the making up after a fight," Aniya added.

Tara and Desiree voiced their agreement.

Heat formed in her belly and spread up to her neck. "Really?"

"Mm-hmm. If you think that fifteen-Mississippi kiss was good, just wait." Aniya fanned herself.

"Okay, let's move on," Stacey said. "Some of us are still single."

They played a few more games, and unsurprisingly, everyone won a prize. The music had shifted to mellow R&B carols, and the five of them fell into their easy rhythm of sharing and encouraging. Monique's mood had lifted, and her future with Alex didn't seem as bleak.

God, thank you for giving me these friends and sisters. May I never take them for granted.

Just as Monique finished one of the best chocolate peanut butter cupcakes she'd ever had in her life, the doorbell rang.

"I wonder who that could be," Stacey said, moving to the door.

"Tell Carl he can't crash the party. Crew members only."

Stacey flicked her wrist. "Please. He and I still hang out occasionally, but not in a you-can-show-up-to-my-house-unannounced way."

When Stacey opened the door, Monique caught a glimpse of Candace, a high school classmate. Her face was puffy, and her arms were wrapped tightly around her waist.

"Candace? Hey girl, what's…" Stacey studied her. "Everything okay?"

"I… I'm sorry. I was just driving and saw your car. I didn't know you had people over."

Stacey waved it off. "You're fine. Come in for a minute. You remember everybody?"

Candace stepped in and looked around the room where Monique, Tara, Desiree, and Aniya gathered. "Oh, wow. Y'all are still hanging together? That's great." She noticed the decorations. "Oh! Y'all are having a party. I'm sorry. I just—I needed to talk for a minute."

"It's fine. have a seat," Monique said.

Candace shrugged out of her coat and slowly sat on the sofa. Her eyes moved from Monique's face to the bride-to-be tiara perched on her head.

"So, it's your night, huh?" she said to Monique with a forced smile. "Congratulations."

Thank you," Monique said, uneasy but polite. "Grab a plate, sit down."

Candace shook her head. "I'm good. Just needed a breather."

Monique and the crew exchanged glances. Then Desiree clapped her hands.

"Okay, it's advice time! Whether you're married or single, everyone can drop a gem for the bride."

They all groaned but circled up anyway.

"I'll go first," Tara said.

"Wait, wait!" Stacey ran to the kitchen and returned with her phone. "We have to record this so Mo can listen to it later."

"Good call," Desiree said. "Make sure to state your

name before you give your advice."

"This is Saturday, December fourteenth, at The Crew bridal shower." Stacey passed the phone to Tara.

"Hey, Monique. This is Tara. My advice is to keep snacks in the house and grace in your heart. It's much easier to be graceful on a full stomach."

Monique chuckled. "You know what? Alex is more easygoing after a good meal." She paused. "And so am I. Thank you."

Tara passed the phone to her right.

"This is Aniya. My advice is to learn to apologize even when you're right. It's cheaper than therapy."

"That one is going to be a challenge for me. I like to be right."

"We know," her friends responded in unison.

She laughed. "It's a good thing that I usually am."

"Whatever," Stacey said and took the phone. "This is Stacey, and my advice to you is to pray more than you plan."

Monique shook her head. "I feel attacked." They all laughed. "You know, I'm a planner."

"Yes, and that's exactly why I said what I said."

She rolled her eyes. "Whatever. Next!"

"Mo, this is Desiree. I have two pieces of advice. The first one is from me. Don't let him 'forget' your anniversary. Calendar alerts save lives."

Everyone—except Candace—laughed.

"These next transformative words were shared with me by a woman who'd been married for over twenty years."

Monique focused on receiving the wisdom, hoping it would be the key to getting her and Alex back on track.

Desiree took a deep breath. "Argue naked."

It was a wrap. Monique collapsed onto the floor, and her entire body shook with uncontrollable laughter. Tears streamed down Tara's face as she gasped for breath. Stacey bent over at the waist, her forehead on her knees as she grabbed her side. Aniya covered her mouth and rocked back and forth as she snorted and shrieked.

"I'm serious. That's what she told me," Desiree insisted through giggles.

Candace sat quietly.

It took a few minutes, but everyone eventually regained control and returned to the circle. Candace reached for the phone and cleared her throat.

"Monique, this is Candace. I know we haven't spoken in years, but my advice is don't rush it. Don't get married because you planned a wedding and everyone is expecting it."

The room went still.

Candace's voice trembled, but she kept going. "I thought if we just went through with it, said the vows, bought the house… we'd be happy. But all it did was give us more rooms to argue in." Her eyes glazed over and brimmed with tears. "Marriage won't fix you, or him. It'll just show you where you're already broken."

Monique's smile faltered. Her stomach twisted painfully. Candace's words were too close, too raw, too true.

Candace shook her head. "I'm sorry, y'all. I… I should go."

No one tried to stop her as she put on her coat and left quietly.

"Well, that was… different," Desiree said. "And it's confirmation of rule number one of our charter. No new members."

The group chuckled, and the mood lightened. But Monique was rattled. Her mind was stuck on Candace's face. The haunted look of someone who'd already lived her worst fear.

Later, after Desiree, Aniya, and Tara left, Monique helped Stacey with the final tidying up. She loaded the empty glasses in the dishwasher, but her mind was miles away.

"You okay, Mo?" Stacey asked gently.

"Of course," Monique said too fast. "This was very sweet and unexpected. Y'all really outdid yourselves."

"We just wanted to celebrate you." Stacey studied her. "Just remember, you don't have to have it all figured out before you walk down the aisle."

Monique looked away and focused on a stray bit of ribbon on the floor. "Yeah. I know." She had at least figured out one thing. "I'm going to head back to the house."

"You sure? You're always welcome to stay here."

"I know, and thank you."

As they hugged, Stacey whispered a prayer. "God, let your will for Monique and Alex be clear. And may they have the courage to go after it."

"Thanks, sis," Monique whispered through her tears.

She hadn't even figured out whether she wanted to stay at Stacey's or go back to the house.

***

The night air bit sharper as Monique loaded her gifts into the backseat—a fancy coffee maker, matching mugs, and a sign that read *Happily Ever After Starts Here*.

She got in and texted Alex.

Monique: The Crew threw a surprise shower. Desiree and Aniya set it up while Stacey, Tara, and I were at BBQ + Blues. It was nice. Hope you got home okay.

Alexander Patterson: Cool. Did you have fun?

Monique: I did.

Alexander Patterson: Monie, I hate when things are tense between us.

Monique: Me, too.

Alexander Patterson: I don't mean to upset you. I just want to take care of you.

She closed her eyes and prayed before she responded.

> **Monique:** I never asked for that, Alex.

> **Alexander Patterson:** Then what do you want?

> **Monique:** I want you to be my partner. Can you do that?

Three dots appeared. Then disappeared. Then finally.

> **Alexander Patterson:** Sleep tight, Monie Love.

He answered her question by not answering it.

As she drove through the quiet Memphis streets, Christmas lights blurred in her vision. Candace's words looped in her head like a song she couldn't turn off.

Marriage won't fix you. It'll just show you where you're already broken.

Monique gripped the steering wheel. For the first time, she admitted it to herself. Not aloud. But deep down, she knew.

If she and Alex couldn't stop breaking each other's hearts before the wedding, what could they promise at the altar?

Chapter 9: Both
In Sickness, In Health

Monday, December 16 — 5 days until the wedding

Monday morning, Alex had the truck's heat on full blast so it would be warm for Monique when he picked her up for their next session with Pastor Cynthia. A faint smile touched his lips. If he'd been asked twenty-four hours prior whether they would be riding together, he would have answered with a resounding no.

What a difference a day makes—and some solid motherly advice.

Even though he enjoyed being with his family and close friends on Sunday, he missed Monique. He felt her absence as strongly as he did her presence when they were together. A piece of him was missing. And his mother picked up on it.

"You've got that Patterson frown. What's wrong?"

He tossed the ball of tangled Christmas tree lights back into the storage bin from which he'd taken them. "I thought we neatly packed these away last year," he said in an effort to channel his frustration onto something tangible.

"I'm not talking about decorations."

His mother sat quietly. It wasn't long before he felt the need to unburden himself.

"Monique and had a disagreement during our session yesterday. And not just yesterday. During most of them." He sighed in frustration. "I'm trying to make sure we're secure, make sure Monique doesn't have to work so hard. But because she took it like I'm telling her to give up her dream, I'm the bad guy."

His mother nodded. "Did you tell her why you want that security? That it's not about silencing her, but about giving her rest?

"Isn't it obvious I want to provide for her? To give her a choice?"

"Alex, you're not giving her a choice if you're deciding it for her."

Even though he was still a little upset and confused, he conceded that his mother had a point. And he couldn't let an entire day go by without at least hearing Monique's voice. So, on his way home, he took his chances and called her.

"Hey, how was the Messiah?"

"Great. How was decorating and dinner?"

"Great."

After an awkward pause, Monique spoke. "We're hanging out at RJ's for a while for dessert and drinks. There's Dad's eggnog and cider, and Mom's coffee. The boys are out of school now, so they're looking for reasons to stay up late. You're welcome to come by."

Alex executed an illegal U-turn and headed to her.

"Who all is there?" he asked as if he cared. Monique being there was all that mattered to him.

"Mom, Dad, RJ, Yvette, Auntie Thelma, and the

boys. Tina and her crew get in on Tuesday."

"Yeah, Kendra, Logan, and the girls get in on Tuesday, too."

"So…you're coming?"

He paused for dramatic effect, even though she probably heard his tires screech. "I'm on my way now."

It turned out to be a pleasant evening. He chuckled. Except for when he asked about the work party.

"The OBS Christmas party is tomorrow night. I signed us up to go. And I know you packed a dress," he said during a commercial break.

She slowly turned her head and raised one eyebrow. "Will Lisa be there?

"Mo, you know HR organizes it."

"Then you already know the answer."

"Are you going to let her ruin what would be a good time? Remember last year? Didn't you enjoy yourself?"

"Yes, that's why the wedding is in that same room." She tilted her head. "I'll make you a deal. If you explain to Pastor Cynthia why I'm against it, we'll go."

Not gonna happen. It was bad enough that Pastor Reginald knew.

"You know, the MMC ice skating and ugly sweater contest is tomorrow night. That sounds like fun, huh?"

"Good idea." She took a sip of her hot cocoa.

Things between them were still a bit fragile, but maybe they were on the mend.

***

Alex and Monique hurried across the First Christian Church parking lot. The cold seeped through his leather, cashmere-lined gloves and bit his fingertips. He grabbed the door handle and ushered Monique inside. His hands tingled as the building's warmth thawed him. They walked down the hall to check in with the receptionist, but were met by Pastor Cynthia in the outer office.

"I'm glad you made it in." She motioned for them to follow her to her office. "That unexpected freeze last night left a lot of people without electricity."

Monique and Alex looked at each other and shook their heads.

"Neither of us had a problem," Alex said.

"We have a tasting at 1:00 this afternoon," Monique said. "I haven't heard anything from them either."

Pastor Cynthia shrugged. "Maybe it was isolated to the downtown area. Okay then, let's get started."

Alex held in his laugh as Pastor Cynthia sat in one of the armchairs, forcing them to nestle on the small sofa.

Fool you once, huh, Pastor Cynthia?

As soon as they were all seated, Pastor Cynthia spoke.

"Today's topic is In Sickness, In Health. It may seem self-explanatory, and admittedly, a part of it is. We'll address that part first, then move into other aspects of the vow."

Getting right down to business. I like your style.

"I hope that you've shared your medical histories with each other and you both know about any underlying or significant health problems."

Alex opened his mouth to speak, but Pastor Cynthia held up her hands.

"I don't need details. I just need an acknowledgement that you have told each other and have heard each other."

"We have," they said in unison.

"Good." She made a note on her digital notepad and then looked up at them. "Vowing to be with someone in sickness and in health is more than bringing them aspirin and chicken soup when they're fighting off the flu."

"We're both healthy. We take care of ourselves and stay active," Alex said.

"He's right," Monique agreed. "And we—"

"Wait," he looked at Monique, "did you just say that I was right?"

"Ha, ha." Monique bumped his knee with hers.

Yep, we're on our way back.

"As I was saying," Monique gave Alex the side eye, then looked back at Pastor Cynthia, "we don't have any chronic illnesses and are doing everything to keep it that way."

Pastor Cynthia exhaled, then smiled indulgently. "That's great, but you're missing the point. We're talking about more than a diagnosis of any sort, whether acute, chronic, or terminal. Every marriage goes through down times. It's called life. And while you are healthy, financially stable people, you're not immune to life."

Alex shifted in his seat. While he acknowledged that illness and economic downturns could—and did—happen, he didn't want to entertain the possibility of a condition that would impair his ability to provide for and protect his family.

"Now, that doesn't mean that God isn't a healer and provider," Pastor Cynthia continued, "but sometimes we have to go through things before it resolves. Sometimes—"

Monique's phone rang. She jumped, then rummaged through her purse to retrieve it.

If she takes a work call in the middle of our counseling session…

"I apologize." She shook her head as she pulled out her phone. "I thought I had it on silent." She turned the phone toward Alex. "It's Elise." She sent the call to voicemail.

She looked up at Pastor Cynthia. "It was probably to remind us of the tasting this afternoon. Again, apologies."

"It's fine. Happens to the best of us. One time, I thought I'd put my phone on silent, and it rang in the middle of Pastor Tony's sermon."

Alex's eyes went wide. "No way!"

She nodded and chuckled. "From then on, I left my phone locked in a drawer in my office."

While he'd initially been a little annoyed when Monique's phone rang, it was a somewhat welcome intrusion. The discussion had him imagining scenarios that rattled him.

"But I digress," Pastor Cynthia said. "Marriage is more than—"

Alex's phone rang. He broke out in a sweat and snatched his phone out of his pocket. "Oops."

Monique's gaze burned the side of his face. He swallowed. She probably caught the look on his face when her phone rang. Now he was the recipient of that some look.

Serves me right. I assumed the worst.

He checked the screen, then looked at Monique. "It's Elise." He turned to Pastor Cynthia. "She did say it was her job to overcommunicate." He silenced his phone. "We'll call her after the session."

"Are there any more phones that need to be checked?"

Alex chuckled. "Since yours is probably locked in your desk drawer, no."

Pastor Cynthia smiled and shook her head.

She likes us.

She picked up where she left off. "Marriage is more than creating and enjoying good times. It's also staying and serving in the hard times." She leaned forward. "In fact, weathering those storms does more to strengthen your relationship than the easy times. Your true selves come out under pressure."

Alex's jaw clenched as flashes of his true self when things went badly with Brionne. Thankfully, he'd grown since then.

Haven't I?

He wrangled his wandering thoughts and tuned back in to Pastor Cynthia.

"'In this life, you will have tribulation. But be of good cheer, for I have overcome the world,'" she quoted. "When you stand before God and pledge 'in sickness and in health,' you're saying that no matter what happens, you'll stay."

Pastor Cynthia paused, but her words hung in the air.

"Today, I want you to imagine and then journal what that vow would cost you to keep. And remember that love isn't always glamorous. Sometimes it looks like staying when you'd rather run, or holding a hand when you can't fix a thing."

Alex looked over at Monique—vibrant, brilliant, and capable. The two of them might not be able to completely misfortune-proof themselves, but together, they could come close.

***

Alex and Monique walked out of Pastor Cynthia's office side-by-side. The counseling session was uncomfortable but bearable. And it was the first session in a while where they didn't argue. Even better, they were on the same page.

Things were looking up.

Alex was glad they had a tasting appointment. He needed something lighter and fun that would erase all the illness- and hardship-talk.

"Oh, hey. Let's call Elise now and let her know we're on our way to the tasting."

"Good idea."

Once the call connected, Monique put Elise on speaker.

"There's no way to do this other than to give it to you straight."

Alex's stomach dropped. *That's not how you want a conversation to start.*

"A major pipe burst at the Peabody. The Skyway ballroom and the entire rooftop area were flooded." Elise sighed before she continued. "It's closed, and there's too much damage for it to be ready by Saturday. All the other ballrooms in the hotel are booked."

Monique's mouth hung open. Tears formed in her eyes.

You gotta be kidding me.

"But don't worry—"

"Don't worry?" Monique's voice trembled. "The wedding is in less than a week, and we have lost our venue."

"The manager at the Peabody and I are on top of it. Between the two of us, we'll find somewhere. And it will be just as nice, if not better, than the Peabody."

Monique closed her eyes and held her forehead. "I guess we should cancel the tasting"

"No, still go."

"For what, Elise?"

Monique was visibly shaking. Alex rubbed her

back, hoping it would soothe her. She didn't pull away or shrug him off.

"The rehearsal dinner isn't being held at the Peabody."

Alex admired how calm Elise sounded.

"But if we can't have a rehearsal, there's no need for a rehearsal dinner," Monique snapped.

The same calmness that Alex admired clearly irked Monique.

"We're working on securing a location," Elise assured her.

"We have only three days, Elise."

"And you only have fifteen minutes to get to the tasting on time. Go." Elise disconnected the call.

Monique was flustered and on edge. He was, too, but he agreed with Elise that they should go to the tasting. The topic of the counseling session was heavy. Good food in a festive atmosphere was just what they needed.

"Monie, I think we should go."

She stared at him, wordlessly.

"Hear me out. The food has already been prepared. Cancelling won't help the situation, but it will hurt *when* we have a new location. And, most importantly, I'm hungry."

She snorted a laugh and shook her head at him. It was the exact reaction he wanted.

"Fine. Let's go."

***

Alex felt slightly off as he and Monique walked to the car.

Maybe I just ate too much.

"So, what did you think?" he asked as he helped Monique into the truck.

"It wasn't bad." She wagged her head. "Actually, most of it was pretty good. But it's your fault that I didn't enjoy it more."

She closed the car door and smiled at him through the window. He jogged around to the driver's side and got in.

"My fault? How?"

"You mentioned that your parents offered to cook. Their food is amazing, so it sets the bar pretty high."

Her teasing him was a good sign. When he smiled, pain shot through his head. He winced then pressed a hand to his temple.

"Headache?"

He shook it off. "Just a little. Maybe too much shrimp dip. But I agree, most of the food was good, but not on the Patterson level. Excluding me, of course. The chicken skewers, however, tasted funny."

"I didn't try them. They didn't look right."

She'd said as much when they were brought to the table, but he thought she was just being finicky.

"Well, have no fear, I didn't select them for the menu."

They rode in comfortable silence for a few minutes. Until he suddenly became very uncomfortable.

Why is it so hot in here? Oh, that's right, I turned it up for Monie earlier.

He turned the temperature down a few degrees.

Hopefully, she won't notice. Or if she does, she won't say anything.

"Are you sweating?" Monique's brows drew together as she studied his face.

Alex touched his forehead. When he pulled his hand away, sure enough, his fingers were wet. He swallowed to counter the queasiness that came out of nowhere.

"You're green around the gills, Alex."

He shook his head. Then pretended it hadn't made his head spin.

"Brown people don't turn green, Monie."

"Fine. You're ashen. If you pull over, I can drive."

"No, I'm okay."

His stomach churned as if it had two elk with locked antlers, fighting for dominance.

I wonder if this is how Rebekah felt when Esau and Jacob tussled inside of her.

"Alex, you're clearly not okay. Pull over." Monique's voice was more forceful, even though it sounded like she was in a tunnel.

The car swayed like a ship at sea. He broke out in a full-body sweat.

Why am I so sleepy?

"Maybe I just need a nap. Yeah, I can just take a quick nap."

His eyelids slammed shut, and his chin dropped to

his chest. The last thing he heard was Monique yelling, "Alex!"

***

Monique parked in front of Alex's condo and looked over at Alex. Was he asleep or praying for the symptoms to subside? After they almost crashed into a median, he finally pulled over, and she managed to help him out of the driver's seat and into the passenger's seat. Alex had at least four inches and thirty pounds on her. In his current, partially conscious state, getting him out of the truck and into the condo would be a challenge. To say the least.

I'll call Marquis. He's just a few doors down.

She checked her watch. It was 4:00 on a Monday. Marquis was at work. She tapped her head against the headrest a few times, praying for an idea to break loose. Calling either set of parents was an absolute no. Alex was her responsibility. They had just talked about that in counseling.

The irony wasn't lost on her. Of course, one of them got sick. Something related to each counseling topic had happened every time. Why would this one be different? They couldn't win for losing.

She didn't know why she was surprised that a pipe burst and ruined the ballroom. Everything around them was bursting—falling apart. They finally got through a session without being at each other's throats, and first the venue turned on them, then the food. The chorus of *God Is Trying to Tell You Something* rang in her head.

But there's no time to wallow right now.

She touched his shoulder and softly called his name. He stirred and groaned.

"Alex, come on. We're going to get you inside."

He grunted. "'Kay."

Her heart clenched. She wished she could make his symptoms go away, but like Pastor Cynthia said, some things you had to go through.

She opened the passenger's door and unbuckled his seatbelt. "Here we go. You ready?"

"Mmm."

That's probably as close to a yes as I'm gonna get.

She put his arm around her shoulders and swung his legs out of the truck.

"You're gonna have to help me a little. Can you stand up?"

Alex lurched forward. Her knees buckled under the initial weight, but she managed to get him to the door, punch in the unlock code on the keypad, and get him to his room. Alex flopped down on the bed. Or maybe she pushed him. Or dropped him. Whatever the method, she had gotten him where he needed to be.

As Alex lay spread-eagled in the middle of the bed, she removed his shoes, socks, and belt. During her debate about how much more clothing she should or shouldn't take off, he bolted upright, wide-eyed, then dashed to the bathroom.

She winced at the torturous sounds coming from the other side of the door. The funny-tasting chicken was making its way through Alex's system. She couldn't tell which end it was coming out of, and that was perfectly fine with her. It was clearly unpleasant either way.

For the next few hours, Alex was in and out of bed, going to the bathroom. After each trip, Monique insisted he sip an electrolyte solution to prevent dehydration. Occasionally, he would eat a saltine or two to help with nausea. And once he took a liquid fever reducer.

She had never been more thankful for 24-hour drugstores and delivery apps. Because Alex had none of those things in the condo.

Men.

Once, while he was out of the room, she searched online whether food poisoning could be fatal.

It could.

The water in the bathroom sink turned off. Alex emerged and shuffled to the bed. She rushed over to help him to bed and forced herself not to react to his drawn face and slow, labored movements. He was a shell of himself.

He searched her face with glassy eyes. "You're shaking."

"I'm fine," she lied.

Seeing him with limp hands and a ragged voice was unsettling in ways she couldn't articulate. Once he settled back into bed, she reached for the cool cloth and pressed it to his forehead.

"It's okay, Alex. Just get some rest."

As he drifted off, she sat quietly beside the bed, one hand resting on his arm, worried about how much it mattered. And when he breathed her name in his sleep, soft and slurred, she felt something she hadn't in years—helplessness.

It was a strong reminder that love carries risks. Because if he could get sick, he could also be gone. That thought burrowed deep and refused to let go. She would be his caregiver in an instant. But she had never considered losing him.

She'd told herself a hundred times that love was about partnership, about two capable people managing life together. But with Alex hollowed out and curled up under a blanket, she realized how fragile that illusion was.

Monique sat there long after he'd fallen asleep, her fingers still tangled with his. Pastor Cynthia's words echoed in her mind. *Sometimes love looks like staying when you'd rather run, or holding a hand when you can't fix a thing.* She'd done both of those.

The time had come for her to go.

Outside, the wind howled. Inside, the room was heavy with the realization that love came with a cost Monique wasn't sure she could bear.

She found a pen and a notepad. Her hand shook as she wrote.

Alex,

Your fever broke a couple of hours ago, but if you feel achy, take one dose cupful of the red liquid. It's fine if you don't want to eat anything, but you must hydrate. It's not optional.

I have to go back to RJ's to shower and change. The Bridal Holiday Tea Party with the church ladies is this afternoon, right after our session with Pastor Cynthia. Assuming we don't need to reschedule.

I'll call in a few hours to check on you.

Love,
Monique

Her hands trembled as she placed the note on the nightstand beside his bed, along with the bottle of acetaminophen, a lemon-ginger electrolyte drink, and saltines. She lingered by his bedside for a few moments, looking at him, loving him. While her heart twisted with all the words she didn't write. Couldn't write.

She kissed his forehead, feeling relieved that he was no longer clammy. He didn't even stir.

Her phone buzzed with a notification that her rideshare driver was one minute away. She moved through the quiet darkness of the condo, got into the back seat of the car, and sent her location to Stacey.

As she rode alone early in the morning, she couldn't shake the fact that she'd only ever thought about being with Alex. She'd never faced the real possibility of losing him. But when she opened herself to love, she also opened herself to loss.

They had been working on how to stay together, but had not prepared to lose each other. Was there a way to do that?

By the time the driver dropped her off, Monique believed losing him on her own terms was better than having him taken away.

Chapter 10: Both
Forsaking All Others

Tuesday, December 17 — 4 days until the wedding

Alex's eyes fluttered open to the soft morning light. His mind was clearer, his body tired but steady. The fever was gone, and the gastrointestinal issues had thankfully ended, but the memory of them stayed.

The night replayed in fragments, but he vividly remembered how Monique trembled as she helped him back to the bed. He'd never seen her afraid before. That look had shaken him more than the illness itself. And he'd been helpless to fix it.

What if the tables had been turned?

He swallowed, trying to banish the image of Monique suffering from an illness. The thought of watching her fade, of being powerless to stop it, was unbearable. He thought he could protect her by planning hard enough, doing enough, earning enough. But no amount of planning could prevent heartbreak. He pressed a hand to his face. Dying didn't scare him. Living without Monique did.

He sat up and looked at the armchair, expecting to see her, but only the neatly folded blanket remained. There was also a note on the nightstand, along with medicine and crackers. He sank into the chair, stared at the note, and took in the faint smell of her perfume that lingered on the cushion.

While he hated being vulnerable and exposed in front of her, he couldn't believe she left. What if he had gotten worse instead of better?

So much for in sickness and in health.

He balled up the note and threw it in the wastebasket. But mere seconds later, he retrieved, smoothed it out, and followed the directions.

As he went to the bathroom to get ready for their final counseling session with Pastor Cynthia, the true meaning of the vow hit him. It meant they would choose each other, even if they could lose everything.

Did he have that kind of faith?

***

Alex's stomach flipped when he saw Monique's car pull into the First Christian parking lot. She stepped out of the car and shook herself, then pulled the belt on her coat tighter. After closing the top button on her coat, she pushed against the wind with her shoulder and rushed toward the door. He stepped away from the window and went to meet her at the door.

Her steps slowed when she saw him. She took him in from head to toe. Then she exhaled and smiled.

"You look a lot better." She took off her overcoat and folded it over her arm.

"You talked to me not long ago."

As she promised in her note, she had called to check on him.

At least I got that much.

"Yeah." She tilted her head. "And you sounded better, and you said that you were good. But I needed to see it with my own eyes."

Then why did you leave?

"Thanks to you." He meant it, even if he was still a little irked that she didn't stay until he woke up. "You look nice."

That was true, too. He'd done some head-to-toe checking out himself. Her high-heeled boots had patches of different shades of brown, and her leather skirt matched the dark brown patches in her boots. The cream V-neck sweater with wide sleeves fit her shape perfectly.

She only had a few T-shirts and sweatpants at the condo. Nothing close to what she wore. Maybe leaving to change was necessary, but he couldn't shake the feeling that there was more to it.

"Thank you." She curtsied.

"You know, this will be your third wedding-related party. I haven't had even one yet." He gave her his best pout and puppy dog eyes.

She shrugged. "You should pick better friends," she said jokingly.

"Hey, my friends are great."

"If you say so."

Monique walked over to Alex and pressed her finger against his bicep to turn him around. Then they went to

Pastor Cynthia's office for their final session with her.

***

Pastor Cynthia sat in one of the armchairs across from Alex and Monique, with her ankles crossed and her hands folded in her lap.

"Our last topic together is Forsaking All Others. It's a promise to give yourself completely to your spouse and to be intimate only with them. But it's also keeping your marriage the primary relationship."

Alex nodded, confident that he had grasped that concept even in his first marriage. While he went about it the wrong way, he cut off communication with Monique to remove all distractions from his relationship with Brionne.

"You gain many wonderful things when you get married. However, to make your marriage a priority, you have to give up some things as well," Pastor Cynthia said.

"Like what?" Monique asked.

"Time, activities, the ability to make decisions in isolation, money, some freedoms, and friendships, to name a few. Today, we're going to delve into family and friend dynamics. How will you manage those relationships?"

We're both close to our families and have close friends who are like family. But they all understand. None of them has ever tried to interfere. They're supportive of our relationship.

Alex decided to start the conversation.

"I always choose our relationship over others."

"Except for when you don't," Monique said, looking straight ahead.

He snapped his head toward her. "Like when?"

"Like Sunday?"

Why is she bringing this up?

"We talked about that."

"No," she countered, "we intentionally didn't talk about it." She threw up her hands. "Face it, Alex. You chose being with your family over being with me."

"Well, you chose *your* family over being with me, too."

She shook her head. "No, you didn't adhere to your own recommendation to either do both activities or trade off. It was a good idea until *you* had to miss *your* family event, since I missed mine last year."

He didn't respond because she was right. What did his reluctance to adjust his family traditions imply for their future?

She continued. "You expect me to do all the giving and sacrificing and compromising. While you get everything you want when you want it. That's not right, Alex."

He scoffed, unwilling to admit the truth aloud. "You're just bringing this up to ease your conscience about last night."

"There isn't anything to 'ease my conscience' about. You were better." She broke their eye contact. "And I needed to get home so that I could dress for the tea this afternoon." She held her hands out to the side to bring attention to her outfit.

"I was wondering why you were so dressed up. Love the patchwork boots and the bell-sleeved sweater," Pastor Cynthia said.

So that's what those sleeves are called.

"Thank you. That's high praise coming from you. Some of the women from—"

"Hello?" Alex interrupted. "We're talking about the fact that you put getting dressed for a tea party over my health."

"Your health?" Pastor Cynthia asked

Monique sighed, then faced Pastor Cynthia. "Alex got food poisoning from the chicken at the tasting."

Pastor Cynthia's voice softened. "Ah. So, you got a real-life demonstration of in sickness and in health."

Monique nodded. "I told him that the chicken was suspect. But he ate it anyway."

Alex jerked upright.

"Is that why you left in the middle of the night? Because you told me so?"

"I left at 5:00 this morning after watching you like a hawk for over twelve hours, wondering whether you were going to get better or die from dehydration." Her voice caught in her throat, and tears formed in the well of her eyes.

I hadn't considered that, but still…

"It's not like last night was a cake walk for me. It was hard, and not just physically." He closed his eyes to keep the feelings of helplessness from surfacing.

"Then," his throat tightened, "I wake up to discover I'm second to your party. Just like I am to your business."

Monique put her elbows on her thighs and dropped her head into her hands. "Not this again." She looked at him. "My business is as important to me as your career and properties are to you. And you work as many long days as I do. Why is it okay for you but not for me?"

Alex shook his head. "It would be okay if you had more of a balance. If we can't figure this out now, what going to happen when we start a family?"

"You say that so casually. As if it's a foregone conclusion." She stood. "What if we aren't able to start a family? It's not guaranteed, you know. And you're oblivious to the pressure that you put on me every time you bring it up."

He shot to his feet. "I never even knew you thought that. This is what I mean about you shutting me out. Starting a family involves both of us, but you just kept that concern locked up inside. How can I support you if you don't tell me things?"

The tension in the air was thick. Their breathing was ragged and shallow.

Pastor Cynthia lifted a hand. "Okay," she said gently. "Take a deep breath, both of you."

Neither did.

Alex opened his mouth, then closed it and shook his head. "You know what, maybe we shouldn't do this right now."

Monique crossed her arms. "No, let's finish it. You clearly have something to say."

"Fine," he said. "You just want someone who won't challenge how you do things."

Her eyes flashed. "And you just want a bondswoman."

He flinched.

"You know what? Why change your name at all?" He flung his arms out to the side. "Just leave it at Lovelace. That's what you really want, right? You as an individual with no obvious ties to me or our marriage? I'm surprised you even wear the ring."

Monique went still, then spoke deliberately. "That can be arranged."

She grabbed the ring, but before she could twist it off her finger, Pastor Cynthia stood.

"Enough." Her voice was calm but unyielding.

They both froze.

Pastor Cynthia rose from her chair and approached them with a steady grace that made people lower their voices without realizing it.

"You two are tired and raw. You're using your words as weapons rather than for communication." She stepped closer, eyes moving from Alex to Monique. "You are not enemies. You are two people terrified of needing each other."

Neither of them argued.

Initially.

"What *I* need is someone who respects me as a person, values my opinion, and allows me to have a life outside of him," Monique said, facing Alex with her hands on her hips.

He folded his arms across his chest. "And what *I* need is someone who will be committed to our relationship and put it first. You know, forsaking all others."

"You mean forsaking anything you disagree with," she retorted.

Monique snatched her coat off the sofa. "I apologize, Pastor Cynthia, but I have to go. This is getting us nowhere."

"How about that?" Alex cocked his head to the side. "We agree on something."

She cut her eyes at him and turned on her heels. Before she could take a step, Pastor Cynthia spoke again.

"Stop. No one is leaving until we pray."

Alex knew that Pastor Cynthia was praying for them and their relationship, but he didn't know the specifics. He couldn't focus.

Because he was suddenly hit with the realization that living without Monique might come sooner than he thought.

***

Monique walked out of Pastor Cynthia's office, down the hall, past the receptionist, out of the building, and right up to the passenger's side of Stacey's car. Without saying another word to Alex. Or even looking in his direction.

She got in and turned to hug Stacey, as much as she could with her seatbelt fastened. Just being in the presence of her best of best friends drained the tension from her body.

"Thank you for picking me. And going to the tea with me."

The Bridal Holiday Tea Party was being hosted by her mother's friends and the church mothers of her and Alex's churches. Stacey had graciously agreed to attend the tea so that there would be at least another person in the same decade as Monique.

"Of course, Mo," Stacey studied her face before pulling off. "Everything okay?"

Nothing was okay. But she decided to just tell her about the burst pipe at the Peabody, meaning they didn't have a location for the wedding. Not that she expected there would be a wedding after their last fight.

"It's the Peabody," Stacey said. "They must have connections somewhere."

After a period of silence and internal debate, she decided to share. If she couldn't tell her bestie, who could she tell?

"Would you hate me if I called off the wedding at the last minute?"

Stacey whipped her head in Monique's direction. "What?"

"Stacey, watch out!" Monique yelled as the sedan swerved into the other lane.

Stacey jerked the car back over the dotted white line. "It's your fault. Why would you say that?"

She recapped their disagreements and how they'd escalated from the first counseling session through the ninth. Hearing herself confirmed her greatest fear. She would either have to lose Alex or lose herself. And she wasn't sure which one would hurt more.

She swallowed to push back the tears. "As much as I care about Alex, I'm not sure if marrying him is the right thing to do."

"You don't just care about him, Mo. You love him."

"But you don't marry everyone you love."

Stacey nodded. "That may be true, but it doesn't mean that you and Alex shouldn't be together." When she stopped at a red light, she looked at Monique. "But to answer your question, I have your back regardless of what you decide. I know what I see from the outside, but you know it all from the inside." She turned her attention back to the road when the light changed. "That being said. I don't think you should worry. Every couple has disagreements. Big ones. These are just bumps in the road."

Monique scoffed. "They feel like potholes big enough to swallow my SUV."

"You have plenty of time to work through this." She steered with one hand and flicked her wrist with the other.

"The wedding is in four days, Stacey."

"Exactly. The Bridal Holiday Tea Party will take your mind off all the negative things and lift your mood. And remind you of everything you love about Alex."

Monique scoffed. "That's a tall order for tea, cucumber sandwiches, and fruit tarts with the church ladies."

It would take a lot more than that to salvage the wedding.

*****

Alex went straight to his condo after the counseling session. Not by his parents' house to see Kendra and his nieces. Not even a call to Marquis. He had to process the past eleven days on his own.

He paced the floor while he deliberated. Monique didn't get it. Putting work first was the death knell for a relationship.

When the constant fighting with Brionne started, they poured themselves into their work to avoid their issues. They would stay apart for days after arguments. No talking and no time together meant there was no way to fix their relationship. Eventually, they had separate lives while still married and living in the same house.

He couldn't let that happen again.

But of course, he couldn't tell Monique. Every time he tried, she accused him of comparing her to his "first wife."

I hate that term.

When he passed the guest bathroom, he couldn't resist turning on the shower. The showerhead that Monique had installed was still there and still functional.

Unlike us.

When he thought about flushing the toilet just to hear the flapper drop, he forced himself to start moving again.

Pitiful.

How could Monique think he wanted to rule over her? He wanted to provide for and protect her, to make life easier for her. He'd been just as insistent on taking pre-marital classes in Atlanta as she was, so they wouldn't end up like he and Brione did.

So much for that.

Hyphenating, shutting him out, putting work before quality time together, and leaving while he was still recovering—all of it added up to one thing: she didn't want him. And he had no intention of staying where he wasn't wanted.

He sank onto the sofa, emotionally drained but fully aware of what he needed to do. A few taps on his phone, and it was finished. He leaned back and drifted into a dreamless sleep.

An hour later, Alex suddenly awoke. Once he got his bearings, he reached for his phone. But there was no response from Monique. He let out a heavy sigh.

Maybe that is her answer.

***

Monique took in the large, three-story home of a former university president and his attorney-wife with wide eyes. It wasn't quite a mansion, but it was as close to one as she'd ever been to. Stacey parked in the circular driveway next to the sign with Reserved for the Bride in cursive letters.

"Wow," Stacey said, staring at the house.

"I know," Monique said. "I'm glad I researched how to dress for a tea party."

"Me, too."

They got out of the car and walked up to the marble steps to the front door. Before Monique could ring the doorbell, the door swung open.

"Miss Lovelace and Miss Witherspoon, I presume," a woman dressed in a smart trouser suit by a designer Monique had probably never heard of.

Monique fought the urge to curtsey. Not a little one like she did when Alex complimented her. But a full one, down to the ground.

Alex.

She wondered what he was doing and whether he even cared what she was doing. Stacey nudged her with her elbow, bringing her out of her thoughts.

"Uh, yes," Monique finally responded. "I'm Miss Patter——," she caught herself, "um, Lovelace, and this is Miss Witherspoon."

"Wonderful. Please allow me to show you to the salon."

Monique's mother, Alex's mother, and the hostess, Attorney Sanderson, greeted Monique and Stacey at the doorway to the salon. After hellos and hugs, they joined the rest of the party.

All the ladies, at least thirty in Monique's estimate, were dressed to the nines in long-sleeved vintage-inspired dresses, flowy silk blouses with long sleeves paired with leather skirts, and knit maxi dresses. And, of course, hats. Banquet tables were arranged in a U-shape and covered with crisp, white tablecloths. Each place setting included a luncheon plate, a cloth napkin, a teacup and saucer, a teaspoon, a spreader knife, a small fork, and a tea strainer. Three-tiered serving dishes filled with a wide variety of savory and sweet treats suitable for proper tea were placed on the tables.

Monique leaned over and whispered to Stacey. "I feel like I'm in a photoshoot for a spread in *Southern Living*."

Her mother escorted her and Stacey to a small square table set for two, placed at the opening of the U. After thirty minutes of sipping tea, eating, and chatting, Attorney Sanderson stood and clapped her hands.

"Ladies, please continue to enjoy the tea and food as we move into the primary reason for this gathering. Monique, as the wife of a man of position, you need to be equipped to entertain properly."

She pressed her fingernails into her palms to keep from laughing.

"So, we have gifts for you to be able to do just that," Attorney Sanderson said. "Naomi. Imogene."

Monique's mother and Alex's mother beamed with joy as they rolled a twelve-foot table filled with gifts next to her.

How much fine China, silverware, and table linens does one person actually need?

Stacey was responsible for recording each person's gift so Monique could send thank-you cards. Monique softly apologized for the dull afternoon they were about to experience.

The first gift was from her first-grade teacher. Monique removed the tissue paper from the gift bag and reached inside. But instead of feeling fabric like cotton or linen, she felt… lace. She peeked into the bag and was stunned by what she saw.

"Pull it out, dear, so everyone can see," her mother said.

Monique vigorously shook her head.

"We'll be here all day," Alex's mother added. "You have a lot of gifts to open."

Not like this one.

Stacey motioned for her to speed up.

Monique sighed and dropped her head. Then she slowly removed two lace bra and panty sets. One red and the other green.

The room erupted in cheers and applause.

"Merry Christmas to Alex," someone said. "He'll love unwrapping that gift!"

"Edna, I almost bought the same thing," someone else commented.

She didn't know who said what because she couldn't look up. The room was filled with her elementary school and Sunday school teachers. Mothers and ministers in the church. Her Girl Scout troop leader. The head of the Youth Ministry and the Vacation Bible School coordinator. She expected housewares and linens.

But she was wrong. *Very wrong.*

Box after box, bag after bag, were filled with silk, satin, lace, and mesh unmentionables - that the women she'd looked up to her whole life had no problem mentioning. In front of her mother! And (maybe) future mother-in-law.

She didn't think it could get any worse than the seven pairs of silk thongs with "Alex" embroidered on them. Until she pulled out a Mrs. Claus teddy.

Her face contorted. "Half of my backside will be hanging out!"

"That's the point, dear," Auntie Thelma said.

God take me now. And comfort Alex when I'm gone. If he still cares.

"You look faint, Monique. You need to eat something. Naomi, pass her a few of those mini quiches. You need to have your strength up for the honeymoon," Auntie Anne said.

The ladies giggled and howled with laughter.

"She's right, dear. I hope you've been exercising," her mother said.

"And stretching," Imogene added. "If Alex is anything like his father, you definitely need to."

Monique didn't know whether to laugh, cry, or run from the room screaming. She thought her mother talking about date nights with her dad was bad. This was an entirely different level. She was mortified.

I can not.

Relief washed over her when she got to the last gift.

Thank God, it's almost over.

It was a contraption made with satin and mesh.

"How do you even put this on?"

"I have no idea," Stacey said, shaking her head.

"I'll show you."

"Mother Johnson!" Monique exclaimed, horrified

"Why do you think Deacon Johnson is smiling every Sunday?"

I can not.

The house manager who greeted them helped Monique, Stacey, Naomi, and Imogene load the gifts into Stacey's car. Once Stacey was in the car and Imogene had gone back inside, Naomi pulled Monique aside.

"Are you okay, sweetheart?"

"Sure, Mom. Once I bleach my brain, I'll be fine."

Naomi chuckled. "That may have been awkward for you—"

"That's putting it mildly."

"But it's also an important part of marriage. It's not the most important thing. But physical and emotional intimacy bond you with your husband." She paused. "But that's not what I was asking." She searched Monique's face. "Are you and Alex okay?"

"Why do you ask that?"

Naomi smiled and put her hand on Monique's cheek. "You're my child. I know you."

Monique's face burned as tears threatened to fall. "I don't know, Mom. I don't know."

Naomi embraced her, and Monique reveled in the comfort only her mother could give.

"Talk to him. And hear his heart more than his words," Naomi whispered in her ear.

Monique nodded.

Naomi released her. "I'm going back inside. Have a good evening."

Monique tilted her head and put her hands on her hips. "Wait, the bride is leaving the Bridal Holiday Tea. Doesn't that mean the party is over?"

"Oh, honey, the party is just starting."

"I can't with you people. We're outta here!"

Monique got in the passenger's seat and looked straight ahead. "We can never unsee that."

Stacey shook her head. "Nope. We're scarred for life."

"We will not speak of this to anyone else for at least five years."

"Agreed," Stacey said and started the car.

They rode in silence for a while. After the shock and horror of the Bridal Holiday Tea Party had faded, the bleak and fragile condition of her relationship with Alex once again took center stage in Monique's mind.

Speaking of Alex.

She unlocked her phone and saw her and Alex's selfie as her wallpaper. Alex was in front, and she was behind him with her chin on his shoulder and her arm wrapped around him. Her hand was on his chest, and her engagement ring sparkled. They were smiling and happy. She remembered that day—they had gone to a Maverick City and Elevation Worship concert.

Where are these two people?

A text from Alex was in her notifications.

Alexander Patterson: We should talk.

She sent back a place and time to meet.

As she brought the gifts inside, Monique couldn't help but think all those ladies had wasted their time and money. Not just because some of those items were so unfamiliar to her that she didn't know what they were, let alone how to wear them. But because judging by Alex's text, the wedding was all but called off.

***

Monique walked through the unusually quiet house to the back porch. Everyone else was at the MMC game night. As she looked out over the back yard, she rolled her shoulders and stretched her neck, preparing for what might be her last conversation with Alex.

It felt familiar. Too familiar.

She dashed up the stairs and grabbed the bag she had packed on Saturday. After adding more clothes, she opened her laptop to search for a hotel room. She had the feeling she would want to be alone after this "talk" with Alex. By a miracle, she found a room so close to Christmas.

She clicked to confirm her reservation, then sent a text to Tina apologizing for disappearing the day she got into town, but she needed a few days of solitude. No further details. Next was a text to Alex.

> **Monique:** Change of plans. I'm coming to you.

She didn't want any more bad memories marring her favorite spot in her childhood home.

Her whole body trembled on the way over to Alex's condo.

This is it.

***

Monique and Alex sat on opposite ends of the couch in his condo. It had been five minutes, and neither of them had spoken since they exchanged hellos when she arrived. Someone had to go first.

"You said we need to talk, but you aren't talking."

He shrugged. "I guess I'm trying to find the words."

She huffed. "You're the one in the rip-the-bandage-off camp."

He gave a weak smile. "I am, usually. I guess I don't want to have this conversation."

"Then I'll start." She took a deep breath. "Everything had been great. Or, at least I thought it was. Then we get these counseling sessions, and we're disagreeing on almost everything." She got up off the couch and paced the small space in front of it. "Were we just putting up a front this past year? Were we both just pretending so we could get to the happy ending that seemed to be right, but really isn't?"

He stood. "I don't think that's it. At least not for me."

She stopped walking and faced him. "Are you saying this is my fault?"

"I'm not laying blame—"

"That's what it sounded like to me."

He raised his hands. "I'm just saying a lot of what you've said during our sessions, I'd never heard before."

"Maybe you just haven't been listening."

"When did you say that you wanted to hyphenate? When did you ever tell me you had concerns about conceiving?"

She didn't answer.

"That's right. Not until less than two weeks," he held up two fingers, "before the wedding. And I'm wrong for being caught off guard about it?"

"I didn't think hyphenating would be an issue for you, so I didn't see a reason to bring it up. And conceiving… is a me issue that I'm working through with God."

He snorted.

"What?"

"It's interesting that you throw God into it, because you know I can't argue with that."

No, he did not.

"You know what else is interesting, Alex? That Lisa felt comfortable enough to buy you underwear."

He spread his arms wide. "How am I responsible for her thinking? You're saying something unreasonable to shift the discussion from what you've done."

"Oh, I'm being unreasonable?" She tilted her head. "How would you feel if one of my male clients bought me underwear?"

His eyes flashed, and his jaw tightened.

"Doesn't sound so unreasonable now, does it, Alex?"

"You said I wanted a bondswoman. Is that what you think of me? That I'm some tyrannical lord who wants to rule over you? That I would misuse the vows of marriage?"

He wasn't going to like what she had to say, but she had to say it anyway.

"It may not be your conscious intention, but you've said it a few different ways. All throughout the sessions, you've talked about providing and protecting —"

"And that's a bad thing?"

"It is when you're using it to try to take something important away from me. You say it's so I don't have to work so hard, but my work isn't a burden. It brings me joy to help small businesses grow. But because you see it as taking time away from you, you want me to cut back or even give it up one day."

He shoved his hands in the pockets of his sweatpants.

"Then you use 'to have and to hold,' 'forsaking all others,' or 'in sickness and in health' to shame me into doing what you want without any consideration for what I want."

He ran his hand down his face. "That's not true, Monie. It is my responsibility to take care of you and provide for you."

"Do I get a say in what that looks like?"

He paced the floor, while she stood completely still.

"What it looks like? Provide, protect, and take care of. Those aren't vague terms. Everyone knows what those mean."

She knew he was talking, but all she could hear were her own words pouring out of her.

"Remember when you asked me what I wanted? I said I wanted us to be partners. You never agreed to that."

"That's a conversation to have in person. Not over text."

An eerie calm came over her.

"It's like you're trying to make me choose. And I shouldn't have to. You can have both. Why can't I?"

He sighed. "You can have both, but you have to give as well as get. Everything can't be your way or no way."

She nodded. The realization hit her like a blow to

the chest. "And everything can't be your way or no way, either."

They were deadlocked, both wanting to get, but neither wanting to give.

Suddenly, her cheeks felt wet. At least, that was how it seemed to her.

"Why are we even doing this?" Monique swiped at her eyes.

"What are you talking about?" Alex's voice was strained.

It had never sounded like that before.

"We don't have a florist, a caterer, or a ceremony location. We disagree on almost everything."

"What are you saying, Monie?"

"I'm saying… I don't know what I'm saying."

"Yes, you do. Say it." He stood in front of her.

She looked up and into his eyes. "Maybe all of these incidents and mishaps… food poisoning, pipes bursting, inappropriate gifts, your guardianship, my conception concerns. Maybe all of this is a sign. Maybe… maybe we shouldn't get married.

"We worked through those."

"Did we? Or did we just put bandages on them and pretend all was well because we have a plan and we want to see it through to the end?"

He knelt down in front of her and took her hands in his.

"I love you, Monique, and I want to be your husband."

Is it the husband I want and need?

"I love you. Alex, and want to be your wife."

Is it the wife you want and need?

"But are we forcing what we want in the face of everything that may be telling us it's not meant to be?"

He caressed her cheek with the back of his hand. "You're just tired and upset—"

She shot up off the couch. "Stop telling me how I feel, Alex! I'm a grown woman. I know my own mind and emotions." She ran her fingers through her hair. "This is why I don't let you in sometimes. You go into fix-it mode when I just need someone to listen. And hear me."

"I was being sincere and trying to find solutions. Apparently, you've just been humoring me." He turned away from her.

"Oh, please, Alex. Always the victim. But you're the one who—"

He spun back around. "Who what, Monie? If you bring up the rift every time, it means you haven't moved past it."

"And you're still trying to deny it ever happened."

A deep, sorrowful groan rose up from deep within her. The realization that they wanted different things and had very different visions for their marriage hung in the air like a heavy load. It was hard to breathe.

He started pacing again. Faster this time.

"It's okay. We can work this out. It's okay."

"No, it's not okay!"

It was as far from okay as it could be.

"Look, I'm not the bad guy here. I'm trying to… I'm trying to…" He stopped pacing and threw up his hands. "What *am* I trying to do? If I have to talk you into going through with this, with us, then maybe… maybe you're right."

Alex flopped onto the couch and held his head in his hands. She knew the feeling.

Monique focused on the wall across the room from her. If she had looked at him, she would have broken.

"Our last session is tomorrow. All three pastors will be there. Let's sleep on it. And pray. If we feel the same way in the morning, we'll tell them then."

***

Monique locked the hotel room door and engaged the safety bar. Walking to the bed took every bit of energy she had. It felt like she was trudging through thick maple syrup. She fell onto the bed and stared at the ceiling as if it held the solution to her problem. But there wasn't one.

She and Alex were breaking up. For real this time. Forever this time.

There wasn't a quick fix to their issues, like dual residence. But it was apparent that last year's "solution" hadn't really fixed anything. Just put a bandage on it. Because they were arguing over the same issues. Alex didn't respect how important her business was to her. It was her purpose, her mission. Her ministry.

She steadied herself and accepted that she wasn't the wife Alex wanted. And she loved him enough to wish for him to get what he desired. Even if it wasn't her. She'd already hurt him. If she stayed with him, she'd only hurt him more.

I'd rather break my own than break his.

Her hand trembled as she tucked her twists behind her ear. Her face burned as a single tear rolled down her cheek. But the shaking intensified as the truth settled in her bones.

Alex and I are over.

Her body convulsed from the force of the sobs that erupted from deep within her. Even after her ducts were drained of tears, she continued to shudder violently.

She wailed and moaned as she mourned the end of a love.

But if they were truly wrong for each other, why did losing him hurt so badly?

Chapter 11: Both
To Love and to Cherish

Wednesday, December 18 — 3 days until the wedding

Alex sat in the same spot on his sofa where he had collapsed the night before, after Monique left. He couldn't bring himself to do anything, not even turning off the lights or changing clothes. The burden of knowing he wasn't the husband Monique wanted weighed so heavily on him that he couldn't stand up. So, he stayed there. All night.

He'd eventually fallen asleep, if startling awake every thirty minutes could be called sleep. But it didn't matter. Nothing mattered. Because he'd run her away. He forced himself to face the harsh reality that they had to break up. If they stayed together, he'd just hurt her more than he already had. He wanted her to be happy. Even if it wasn't with him.

Alex's joints popped, and his muscles cramped as he slowly rose. But the pain in his body didn't compare to the pain in his heart from losing his Monie Love.

But I'd rather break my heart than hers.

***

Alex avoided Monique's eyes when they met at the

entrance of Grace Life Church, and she did the same. She mumbled a greeting, and he grunted one in return. Then they entered the building. On the silent walk to the counseling room, he felt like a condemned man heading to his doom. Probably because that's exactly what he was doing.

They greeted each of the Pastors, then sat as far apart as the loveseat allowed. When they finally made eye contact, Alex could tell by the look on Monique's face that they'd come to the same conclusion. They had to break up. Their silent nods to each other spoke volumes.

Alex took a deep breath before delivering the news. "We… talked last night, and—"

"Stop." Pastor Cynthia held up her hand."

Monique drew in a quick breath. The hardness in her voice, posture, and eyes surprised him, too.

"Over the past nine sessions, you two have done a lot of talking, some hearing, but very little listening." Pastor Cythia turned her palms up. "So, in this final session, you aren't talking—only listening. And do so the way you want to be listened to."

Alex swallowed at the sting of the reprimand, but he didn't dare to object. Monique stiffened but stayed silent.

Pastor Mike peered at them over the rim of his glasses. "To love and to cherish is a promise to recognize your spouse's value and to sacrifice for them."

I'm already sacrificing myself so that she can find

someone she can be happy with. What more can I give?

"Self-sacrifice." Pastor Mike looked at Monique. "Are you ready to give up the life you've built for yourself," he turned to Alex, "or imagined that you'd build together?"

She shifted in her seat. He looked down at the floor, feeling sufficiently rebuked.

"You have been protecting yourselves instead of opening up and being vulnerable with each other. You've been working so hard to convince the other that your way is the only right way and that it's *the* way that it has to be."

Pastor Mike's lips curved into a small smile. "But you're missing the fact that you'll each change and grow and discover things about each other for the rest of your lives. You can't put yourself or your spouse in a box."

Pastor Reginald slid forward in his chair. "The purpose of premarital counseling isn't to identify and solve all your challenges and issues. It's to shine a light on the fact that you have differences. So, if you're expecting to agree on everything and do everything the same way…" He shook his head. "Well, that's boring and unproductive. You need different perspectives. If you both think alike, when you get stuck, there is no way out."

Pastor Reginald's words made sense and challenged Alex to reflect on his behavior and demands. But he still wasn't completely convinced that he and Monique could make it work. He glanced at her out of the corner of his eye. She faced front and sat completely still, her spine ramrod straight.

Maybe this isn't as difficult for her as it is for me. Maybe it's a done deal for her. Maybe just doesn't want—

Monique tugged her ear.

She did that whenever she was uncomfortable. It took a lot of effort for Alex not to smile. While it didn't necessarily mean they would reconcile, it did mean they were both at least examining themselves.

Pastor Reginald continued. "Over these two weeks, you've heard some things you haven't heard before and learned some things you didn't know. And, let's just be honest, some of that you don't like. But what are you going to do?"

He paused and let the question sink in.

"Do you bail and go on the unrealistic quest to find someone who doesn't challenge you? Or do you choose someone who supports you in uncharted waters?" He looked at Monique. "Like fixing a toilet," he turned to Alex, "or cooking a meal."

Touché, Pastor Reginald.

Our goal," he gestured to Pastors Mike and Cynthia, "was to give you tools to navigate differences in opinions and expectations that can lead to disagreements. So that, eventually, you use your different approaches, ideas, and strengths to make better collective decisions." He laced his fingers together.

Pastor Cynthia took the lead. "We want to leave you

with five key points that sum up what we've discussed during our sessions. Number one, love alone won't keep a marriage alive. Commitment, effort, and willingness to adapt are necessary to sustain it. Number two, conflict is not only unavoidable but also vital because it brings issues to the surface. Fighting does not damage the relationship. It's how you manage, or mismanage, disagreements that causes problems."

"Number three," Pastor Mike said, "Your spouse won't and can't meet all of your needs. Only God can. Number four, marriages, like every other relationship, don't magically stay in good shape. They have to be maintained with regular check-ins and quality time together. There is no autopilot for a marriage."

"And number five, you're both going to change. So, embrace it rather than resist it. Adapt and grow together," Pastor Reginald added.

Whew.

They gave Alex a lot to think about. His parents made it look easy, but they clearly did a lot to keep their relationship strong, something he never noticed or considered.

Pastors Mike, Cynthia, and Reginald stood.

There's more?

"Our purpose wasn't to give you a stamp of approval and declare you 'ready.' But for you to take an honest look at yourself, your partner, and what it takes to have a happy marriage—the work you have to put in." Pastor Cynthia's voice was softer than when they started the session.

Hopefully, that's a good sign.

"We love you and want the best for you. But you have to decide if this is the relationship you want to make work. So, what's your honest answer? When the newness fades, and the fantasy of marriage gives way to the reality of marriage, will you do the work to make it last?" She held up her hands. "Don't answer that now. Because you need to hear what God is saying. When you came in this morning, prepared to make an announcement, were you listening to God or to your hurt feelings?"

Pastor Cynthia's words hung in the air like a cloud heavy with rain before a severe thunderstorm. Alex broke eye contact, and Monique pulled her ear.

"Go home, pray, and listen to what God is saying about getting married. Not you, your family, or your friends. Stay apart from each other with no contact for the rest of today and tomorrow. Use that time to hear and be sure of how God is leading you. Then write an open, completely honest letter to each other about your decision. On Friday, come together and exchange letters."

Monique spoke for the first time. "But that's the day before the wedding."

"We know. We're officiating," Pastor Reginald said.

Monique wordlessly stared at the three pastors in disbelief.

"What's more important?" Pastor Cynthia asked.

"Saving face or following God?" Pastor Reginald finished.

Pastor Mike signaled for them to stand. The five of them linked hands, and each pastor prayed for Alex and Monique's hearts to be healed, for their ears to be open to God's voice, and for them to have the courage to follow God's guidance.

We're going to need it.

***

Once again, Monique was glad she had a hotel room. There was no way to explain Alex's two-day absence to her family. And with her brother, sister, brother-in-law, sister-in-law, three nephews, and niece in the house, she would barely have two minutes alone, certainly not enough time to pray about a decision that would literally affect the rest of her life.

Her phone buzzed again. It was the third text message from Elise, after two phone calls that Monique sent to voicemail. How could she explain the current situation?

"Um, hi, Elise. Yeah, the wedding you've been planning for the past eight months might not happen. But I won't know for sure until the day before." She shook her head. "I'm not having that conversation."

But ignoring her calls was unprofessional. She contemplated what to say, and finally settled on a short text message.

Less is more.

Monique: I'm unavailable. We'll talk on Friday.

It was lame, but the best she could do at the time.

Elise wasn't the only person reaching out to her. The bridesmaids, her parents, Alex's mom, aunts, and cousins—all were in contact. She messaged her mother and Stacey, telling them she was fine but that she had to handle something very important. Alone. Then she put her phone on silent.

Hopefully, they will communicate with everyone else.

She put a pillow at one end of the small sofa, then reclined on it and clutched another pillow to her chest. After staring at the ceiling for a few moments, she gave in to the heaviness that had been on her since she awoke and closed her eyes. A long exhale escaped through her mouth.

The past twelve days played like a movie in her mind. Seeing herself from the outside gave her a completely different perspective of herself and Alex. The first tear fell when the scenes shifted to the past eight months of their engagement. By the time she watched her and Alex reconnect during the previous Christmas and finally admit their love for each other, her cheeks and chin were wet.

Her visual journey continued through graduate school, college, high school, and even the day they met in middle school. And the whole time, Alex was there supporting her, providing for her, and protecting her in ways she'd never realized until that moment.

Monique tossed the wet pillow to the floor and prayed. She thanked God for His patience and love. For showing her Alex's heart. And for allowing her to be loved by Alex. She prayed that Alex would forgive her. That she would have the courage to tell him that she loved him. And that she would never allow the depth of her love to scare her again.

When Monique opened her eyes, she was on her knees, and it was dark. What felt like minutes had been hours. She looked down at her rumpled, wet shirt and tried to remember when she had changed clothes. As she pushed off the edge of the sofa to stand, she smiled because she had her answer. But her smile faded by the time she was on her feet.

Would Alex's answer be the same as hers?

***

Alex silenced his phone after getting another text from Elise. There was only one person he wanted to talk to, and she wasn't allowed to speak to him for another day and a half. If she even wanted to. On top of that, Elise's only topic of discussion was the wedding. That might not happen. She would just have to wait.

However, he couldn't completely ignore Kendra or his adorable nieces. Still, Uncle Alex wasn't in a good mood. He'd only ruin their Christmas cheer. So, he sent Kendra a text saying he'd be busy with wedding stuff until the next day.

That should buy me some time.

His heart ached as he thought back on the charge he'd been given. *Pray and listen to what God is saying about getting married. Be sure of how God is leading you.*

He hadn't prayed yet. What if God said what he didn't want to hear? His stomach clenched at the thought of it.

While he had previously resigned himself to breaking up with Monique, he didn't truly want to. If she had shown even the slightest hint of wanting to stay together, he would have taken it. But why would she have?

They were having the same argument as Christmas before. He wanted everything his way and was trying to control everything to avoid getting hurt. The pastors had named it—selfishness and fear.

He was back full circle. The same issues that cost him their relationship were back at it again. With the same results. When would he learn?

I can start today.

"God, please show Your will concerning me and Monique."

Their arguments from the counseling sessions and the year before played in his head. He winced at the things he said and did.

"Even though I sometimes let selfishness and fear get me into trouble, I love her and want to spend the rest of my life with her." He swallowed to clear the lump in his throat. "Help me show her the love You show the church, sacrificing and caring for her. Not controlling and limiting her out of fear."

Something inside him broke. Not a damaging break, but a breaking free. He had his answer. And he couldn't have been happier.

"Thank You for bringing us together. Thank You for forgiveness. Thank you for another chance. And thank You for Your love, my love for Monique, and prayerfully, her love for me."

Chapter 12: Both
To Love and to Cherish?

Thursday, December 19 — 2 days until the wedding

Monique pressed her thumbnail between her teeth as she paced the hotel room on Thursday afternoon. She was supposed to be writing her letter to him. Instead, she worried that he would decide being with her was too complicated.

There was probably a line of women eager to accept the life he offered.

Lisa would be in the front.

She rolled her eyes at the thought. Although Monique forgave Lisa for crossing the line, she was still uninvited.

Her thoughts returned to Alex. Maybe she could blame her behavior on wedding jitters. Would a letter begging him to take her back be pathetic? She ran her hands through her hair and released a groan of frustration. She knew Alex's heart. How had she ever thought otherwise?

Another stray thought crossed her mind. In the time they had been apart, nothing else had gone wrong with the wedding. But then again, what more could have happened?

A call on her business line stopped her in her tracks.

Her finger hovered over the button to send the unknown number to voicemail. It could have been a potential new client, or a florist Jess had contacted. Not that she was in the headspace to woo a new client. And she might not even need a florist. Yet, against her better judgment, she swiped to answer.

"Empower PR Partners."

"Monique Lovelace."

Justin's distinctive drawl filled the air.

This is what I get for ignoring my first instinct.

"Justin. To what do I owe this unexpected… call?"

He chuckled. "You always did have a quick wit. I heard that you're getting married. I was so surprised that I had to confirm the rumors were true."

Seriously?

"Considering our history, I didn't think you were willing to make the sacrifices needed to be a wife."

His jab added to her anxiety. It was exactly what Pastor Mike had said the day before. *To love and to cherish is a promise to recognize your spouse's value and to sacrifice for them.*

"But," Justin continued, "I suppose all the years being single could have made you realize the error of your ways."

His parting words came back to her: *Before you decide you're done with us, ask yourself one question. In ten years, which will you regret more—not starting a business or not getting married?*

Then she recalled Alex's evaluation of Justin, and it eased her insecurities.

"Actually, it's because I'm marrying someone who isn't insecure, immature, or threatened by my success." The pressure in her chest eased.

"You have the right to want what you want in a relationship, Justin. And I have the right to want what I want. What each of us wants is very different. That doesn't make either of us wrong. But it does mean we are wrong for each other."

Her thoughts became clearer. "The problem was that you weren't truthful about your expectations. And you tried to make me feel that what I wanted was wrong. Tried to shame me into giving up the life I wanted to give you what you wanted."

She considered doing a cartwheel but decided against it since she hadn't done one in nearly twenty years.

"Interesting," he drawled. "Who's the lucky guy anyway?"

"Alex Patterson." Saying his name made her smile.

"Alex? The one who was married? Your friend who ghosted you? If he divorced his first wife, what makes you think it's going to work with you?"

Time to end this.

"Are you married, Justin? If so, why are you spending time talking to me instead of your wife?"

Silence was the only answer to her question.

"Ah, you're not married. Well, enough said. This has been… interesting, but I have to go, Justin. I'm getting married in two days." *Hopefully.* "Have a good life."

Monique disconnected the call and grabbed a pen and a notepad. She finally knew exactly what to say.

***

On Thursday afternoon, Alex recapped the final counseling session to Marquis. He hadn't planned on telling anyone about it, but after he hadn't gone to spend time with his sister or nieces, his mother called Marquis and insisted he find out what was going on. Marquis, not wanting to lose his regular invitation to Sunday dinner, agreed.

"So, you don't love Mo anymore?"

What is wrong with him?

"Of course, I do."

Marquis cocked his head to the side. "Oh, you love her, but you don't want to marry her?"

This dude.

"I want to marry her more than anything."

"Okay," Marquis drew out. "So then, the disagreements and the things that have gone wrong mean God is telling you she's not the one?"

Alex sprang up from the recliner. "Why do you keep asking me these ridiculous, inane questions?"

Marquis leaned back on the sofa and put his ankle on the opposite knee. "Because, to quote a great philosopher, 'It's déjà vu all over again.' This is exactly where you were last year. Knowing what you want, but not fighting for it."

"I can't make her want me, Marq."

Marquis shook his head and stood. "You don't have to because she already does. You're both aware, and a little apprehensive, of the depth and breadth of the commitment. Because they're huge, and you both want to get it right. But the fear of messing up is trying to keep you from your destiny." He paused. "What does the Word say about fear?"

"'God has not given us a spirit of fear, but of power, of love, and of a sound mind,'" he quoted 2 Timothy 1:7.

"You alone are impressive. Mo alone is a force to be reckoned with."

Alex couldn't help but smile. *That she is.*

"The two of you together…"

We'd be unstoppable.

"Let me ask you this, Alex. Do you think you'd be facing so much opposition if your marriage wasn't going to change lives and the world?"

Alex lightly punched Marquis's shoulder, then walked him to the door.

"Thanks for stopping by, Marq. I have a letter to write."

Chapter 13: Both
All the days of my life

Friday, December 20 — The day before the wedding

On Friday morning, Monique took the elevator down to the lobby to meet Alex at 9:00. She sent him a meeting invite at 12:01 AM, adhering as closely as possible to the no-contact-for-two-days rule.

A morning meeting made the most sense. They could have breakfast, although she was too nervous to eat. She could check out early, even though her rewards status automatically granted her a late check-out. But the real reason was that it gave them more time to cancel the wedding activities if needed. She prayed they wouldn't have to. The thought alone made her queasy.

As soon as she got off the elevator, she scanned the lobby. At no sign of Alex, she checked her watch. 8:59. She took a breath to slow her wildly beating heart.

Calm down. He's not late.

At 9:05, she checked her phone for any messages. She decided to relax in one of the lounge chairs to stop her fidgeting. But as soon as she sat down, she popped right back up. At 9:10, she willed herself not to cry and walked toward the elevators. Not only was Alex not going to marry her, but he wasn't even going to show up.

"Monique!"

At 9:11, she heard her name. She slowly turned toward the auditory hallucination and saw Alex sprinting across the lobby.

No hallucination. He's here!

He reached her in seconds.

"I'm so sorry. I had to go back home to get something, then ran into traffic. Did you know they are doing construction on 240, again?" His words rushed out amid heavy breaths. "Sorry," he shook his head, "I'm rambling, but I'm here. I'm here, Monique."

"I thought you weren't coming."

"And have to answer to Pastor Cynthia?" He vigorously shook his head. "No, thank you."

She laughed lightly, still trembling with relief.

"Seriously. I apologize for being late." His chest was still heaving.

"It's okay, Alex. Catch your breath."

She led him to two plush lounge chairs in a small corner off the lobby. After they sat down, they simply looked at each other. It was so wonderful to see him. Two days had felt like two years. She broke eye contact before she teared up again and reached into her handbag.

"I have my letter."

Alex pulled an envelope from his backpack. "I have mine, too."

Monique sighed. "Okay. I'm going back upstairs to read. This is a low-traffic area, so you'll have privacy and space."

His eyes widened. "Go upstairs? You have a room here?"

"Yeah, I checked in on Tuesday night. After we…"

She couldn't bring herself to say it.

"Right." He nodded.

She thought she saw regret in his eyes, but it might have been wishful thinking.

"I needed space to think. It's hard to get that with eight other people in the house."

"That's right, Tina and her family are here."

He remembered.

"Yeah. And Kendra and family came in." She shook her head. "Ella has probably already asked about Hailey and Leigha."

He huffed a laugh. "Yeah. They've probably asked about her, too."

Will they get the chance to see each other?

They were hesitating, but they had to confront their moment of truth.

"Well," she slapped her hands on her thighs and stood.

He stood, too. "I'll, uh, see you in a few."

Alex walked Monique to the elevator. It dinged, and the doors swished open. She stepped inside and turned to face him. He locked eyes with her for a second, then looked away. Monique exhaled the breath she was holding.

Just before the doors closed, a hand was pushed into the small gap, and the doors reopened.

"What's your room number?" Alex asked as he held the doors open.

"718."

"I'll come up… when I'm done."

She was encouraged. "Okay. See you then?"

"See you then."

Alex released the doors, and they swished shut. Monique turned the envelope over in her hand as she rode the elevator to discover her future.

***

Alex watched the elevator close and take the woman he loved away. He watched the numbers above the door until the seven lit up, paused, then dropped back down to the lobby.

Her giving him her room number was a good sign. If her letter told him to jump off a cliff and take his controlling ways with him, she wouldn't let him come up. Right? But she hadn't told him she was staying at a hotel. However, they weren't really speaking on Wednesday morning, and they were told not to contact each other for two days. So, she couldn't have told him. Maybe it wasn't as bad as he thought.

He grunted in frustration. *Just man up and read the letter!*

After settling back into the chair he'd left, Alex prayed for wisdom and acceptance. Then he opened the envelope.

My Dearest Alexander Patterson,

It scares me, Alex, to think that the life I've known and built and lived is going to change so drastically. But I'm willing to do it, even if I have to do it afraid. I don't want to keep the life I have if you're not in it. Because I believe you're the man God has for me.

You can be on any account I have because I trust you to do right by me and for me.

No matter what my name is, you have my heart.

Even though you drive me nuts when you leave your shoes in the middle of the floor, I'd rather be irritated with you than without you.

I spent so long trying to be strong that I forgot love also needs softness. You try so hard to protect me that you forget love needs trust. Maybe the only way forward is for us both to lay those burdens down.

It's not going to happen overnight, but if you're willing to work with me, I'm willing to work with you. That's all I ever wanted.

So, here's my decision: I choose you, Alex. Not because I'm sure it'll be easy. But because even in the hardest moments, when everything falls apart, you're still the person I want sitting beside me.

Love always and forever until the end of time,
Monie Love

***

Monique had sat on the sofa, then the bed, then the chair, then went back to the sofa.

"Oh, stop it! Just read the letter!"

Her hands trembled as she lifted the flap of the envelope. She paused before unfolding the letter.

"Thank you, God, that no matter what it says, You've got me."

My Monie Love,

I realize now how much of my love has been about control. If I keep the house running, the bills paid, the plans clear— maybe nothing can fall apart. I was so caught up in not repeating my past mistakes that I forced on you what I thought would please you. But I should have listened to you, heard what you needed, and given you what you wanted.

I finally understand that there are no rules about what a wife wants, other than to listen to what my wife is telling me and respond (and NOT being given boxers from another woman).

I never meant to make you feel that I was comparing you to anyone else. Because nothing and no one compares to you. I'd rather spend every day of the week arguing with you than see everything go my way without you in my life.

I accused you of being unwilling to sacrifice for the relationship, even though I wasn't either. But I'm ready now.

I can't promise perfection, but I can promise persistence. I want to live this life with you. Enjoying the victories, enduring the losses, and looking back on a lifetime of love conquering all.

I choose you. Every messy, uncontrollable, beautiful part of you.

I want you to be my wife, Monie. And I want to be your husband.

If you'll still have me, I'm all yours— with reckless abandon.

Love always and forever until the end of time,
Alexander

Monique wiped her eyes and whispered, "Thank you, God."

Loud, insistent knocks on the door jolted her to her feet.

What in the world?

She looked through the peephole, then grinned. Alex was breathing hard and smiling.

Did he take the stairs?

She flung open the door.

"Are you done reading? Tell me you're done reading."

"I'm done reading."

"Thank God!"

Alex entered, closed the door, and pulled Monique into his arms in one smooth motion. She relaxed into his hold, finally at peace after three days of chaos.

He broke the hug by extending his arms with his hands on her shoulders. "I need to tell you why I was late."

She shook her head. "I don't care, Alex. What matters is that you're here now."

He stepped back and reached into his backpack.

Is he getting what I think he's getting? She bounced on her toes.

"I had to go back and get this."

He displayed the Simba figurine that she had given him in high school. She squealed and hurried to her duffel bag, showing him the Nala figurine he had given her in exchange. He placed Nala and Simba on the coffee table. His arms slowly wrapped around her waist, and he pulled her close. She rested her head on his chest, and his heartbeat echoed through her as they swayed to music only they could hear.

Another knock on the door jarred them apart.

Who could that be?

"Did you order room service?" Alex asked.

"No."

"Are you expecting someone?"

She shook her head. "No one else knows I'm here."

"Wait here."

Alex went to the door and checked the peephole. "Of course."

He opened the door, and Elise strode in.

"The polite and professional thing to do when your wedding planner calls and texts you is to respond."

Monique opened her mouth, but Elise continued before she could get a word out.

"And not with, 'We'll talk on Friday.'"

"How did you find us?" Alex asked.

"I have my ways." Elise flicked her wrist. "But that's not the point. We have a wedding tomorrow!"

Monique and Alex grinned.

We most definitely do.

Elise flipped open her tablet. "I know the Peabody was your first choice, but we got the Pink Palace Mansion at the Museum of Science and History. You and your guests will be able to visit the Enchanted Forest and take pics. It's going to be perfect. The Pebody is going to shuttle over the guests staying there, and we've sent out communications to everyone who RSVP'd."

Monique got teary. After they broke up the past

Christmas, they ran into each other at the Enchanted Forest. She looked at Alex. Even his eyes were a little watery.

"Each of you will be driven to the Pink Palace Mansion for the rehearsal at 5:00. Then you'll be taken to a different location for the dinner," Elise said.

"Why are we being driven by someone else?" Monique asked.

"Where is the dinner going to be?" Alex asked.

Elise looked up from her tablet. "Oh, now you want all the details after ignoring my calls and texts for three days?"

"Elise, I—"

She held up her hand. "It's okay, Monique. You're not the first bride and groom to disappear for a few days. I would have liked a bit of a heads-up, but I get it."

"Thank you. Can I ask who's catering the rehearsal dinner?"

"Well, not the people who poisoned, Alex. That's for sure. Trust me. You're going to be pleased."

Monique's initial instinct was to protest, but she decided to take the first step in not doing everything herself.

"I believe you. Elise." Alex looked at her in surprise, then nodded his head.

"What else do we need to know or do?"

Elise handed each of them a schedule. "Be at these places at these times with yourself and the items listed. Everything else has been taken care of."

***

As instructed, Monique was "dressed cute" and ready to be picked up by 4:15 PM. Tina and Yvette, also dressed cute, joined at the front door just as the doorbell rang.

Monique opened the door to find a chauffeur on the doorstep and a stretch luxury SUV in the driveway. She looked at Tina and Yvette, who just smiled at her.

"Miss Lovelace?" the chauffeur asked.

"Until tomorrow," Monique said.

"Your ride awaits."

He gave her his arm and escorted her down the steps and to the SUV. Inside were the rest of her bridesmaids—Stacey, Tara, Desiree, Aniya, Jessica, and Kendra.

This is too much!

"No ma'am! No tears. It's time to party!" Stacy ordered.

***

The rehearsal went without a hitch, and before Monique knew it, they were back in the SUV on the way to the rehearsal dinner.

Wherever that is.

Once they pulled into the parking lot, Monique knew exactly where they were going.

"The Christmas Store. Of course."

If she and Alex hadn't volunteered to work at the

Christmas Store for the Merry Memphis Christmas Festival the year before, they would not be a day away from getting married.

Just as her driver stopped at the curb, another stretch SUV pulled up behind them.

Must be Alex and the groomsmen.

Alex got out first and sauntered over to Monique.

She put her hands on her hips. "Did you know about this?"

"No. I was going to ask you about it."

They walked inside, hand-in-hand.

Something smelled familiar to Monique. She sniffed the air, turned to Alex.

"It can't be."

He inhaled and smiled. "I think it is."

Alex's parents came over to them.

"We couldn't cook for your rehearsal dinner and not make your favorite dish, Monique," Thomas said, smiling.

Monique shimmied and sang. "I'm gonna have some pasta bake. I'm gonna have some pasta bake."

And she did.

The rehearsal dinner ended up being even better than she had anticipated. People shared stories about her, Alex, and their relationship. Nearly everyone there mentioned they'd known for years that the day would come when they got married. Apparently, she and Alex were the only two who remained unaware until decades later.

But better late than never.

Alex and Monique stole away to the storage room as the dinner was winding down. She reached up and laced her fingers behind his neck. He took her by the waist and pulled her to him.

"You ready?" He asked.

"Absolutely positively."

His gaze dropped to her lips. "You know, this may be our last kiss as an engaged couple."

"Then we'd better make it a good one."

And boy, oh, boy, was it. The touch of his lips on her mouth sent her stomach into a wild swirl, and she sank into a dreamy intimacy. Feeling as if she was floating, she eagerly returned the kiss. Alex was her past, present, and fut—

"Alright, break it up," Marquis demanded as the metal door groaned open.

Alex and Monique jumped apart.

"That's right," Stacey said. "Time for part three of the evening. Alex, you'll see her again when she's walking down the aisle."

Marquis handed Alex a handkerchief and gestured for him to wipe his lips. Stacey grabbed Monique by the hand and pulled her from the storage room.

Monique and Alex got one last look at each other as they were ushered into their respective stretch SUVs and whisked away to their bachelor and bachelorette parties.

Which they both thoroughly enjoyed and promised that what happened in Memphis…

Chapter 14: Both
I Do

Saturday, December 21 — Wedding Day!

The piano and cello started the opening notes of Pachelbel's Canon in D. The gentle melody drifted through the vaulted space. Monique took a deep breath and tightened her grip on her father's arm. The warm scent of flowers greeted her as Stacey handed her the bouquet. Thanks to Elise's persistence, Blooms by Bethany had delivered every one of the flowers she had chosen months ago.

Red amaryllis, white carnations, gerbera daisies, tulips, gardenias, and delicate paperwhites. Every petal carried a meaning: love, loyalty, worthiness, forgiveness, joy, hope, and devotion. They told the story of their love journey better than words ever could.

The doors opened, and sunlight poured through the tall windows of the Pink Palace Mansion, glinting off strings of tiny white lights that wove through the rafters. Her heart skipped a beat as she took in the unexpected beauty of the space, where the Christmas before they ran from each other, and a year later, they were running to each other.

The Pink Palace and the Enchanted Forest were never even considered as wedding venues. And yet, standing at the edge of the aisle on her father's arm, surrounded by love, and knowing Alex waited for her, it was the perfect place.

This was not what we planned. It's better.

Halfway down the aisle, she saw Alex. Her breath caught in her throat. The tuxedo fit him perfectly, but it was the look in his eyes that undid her—steady and full of love. His eyes locked on hers, and something inside her settled. Every change in plans, every detour, every mishap had led to this one moment.

Pastor Cynthia stood at the altar. Pastor Mike and Pastor Reginald were on either side of her. All smiling like proud parents.

When Monique reached the end of the aisle, her mother stood next to her father, and they lifted her veil together. Her mother kissed one cheek and said, "I love you." Her father kissed the other and said, "I'm proud of you." Then they took their seats, and Monique joined Alex at the altar.

Pastor Mike cleared his throat softly, his eyes twinkling. "Well, now that we've all survived the venue change and a tasting that will never be spoken of again…" Laughter rippled through the crowd. "Let's celebrate what this day really means."

"Love," Pastor Reginald said, "is about persistence, not perfection. God weaves beauty out of chaos when we stop trying to control things. Because sometimes He lets things fall apart so they can fall into place."

The crowd nodded and murmured their agreement.

Pastor Cynthia officiated as Monique and Alex vowed to have and to hold, for better, for worse, for richer, for poorer, in sickness and in health, to forsake all others, to love and to cherish all the days of their lives.

And they meant it.

***

Alex reveled in the time he had alone with his wife while the wedding party was introduced at the reception. His appreciation for a large wedding party grew. Soon, he'd be pulled into all the activity of the reception. But at that moment, it was just him and his wife, Monique.

I'm so glad to be able to call her that finally.

"Alex!" Monique clutched his arm. "We never practiced our dance!"

They had planned to dance to *Wifey* by Next, but he had a surprise for her.

He put his arm around her and kissed her forehead. "Don't worry about it. Just follow my lead." He grinned and winked at her.

She shook her head and smiled. "What am I going to do with you?"

"I still have that list of suggestions."

She bumped him with her shoulder. "Later."

"Ladies and gentlemen, get on your feet, and welcome Alex and Monique Patterson!" Elise said into the mic.

Alex stopped and looked at Monique. She smiled and shrugged. "It's negotiable."

They entered to applause and cheers. Alex turned her, then pulled her close and signaled the DJ to start the music. A familiar, soulful intro poured through the speakers. Monique froze as recognition dawned.

"It's *I Believe in You and Me* with Levi Stubbs. You changed it?" she whispered.

He nodded and spoke softly. "Our first date. Our first dance. Seemed right to start forever with it too."

The guests melted away as he drew her into his arms. She rested her head against his chest. The lyrics wrapped around them like a blanket that would cover them for the rest of their lives—believing in the miracle of love.

They were Alex Patterson and Monique Lovelace-Patterson.

Two perfectly imperfect people who were perfect for each other.

Epilogue: Monique
From This Day Forward

Fifteen years later…

Monique and Alex sat side by side, hands clasped together, fingers interlaced—the same way they had been on that December day when they promised forever. Across from them, a young couple perched on the loveseat in the Counseling Center, wide-eyed and nervous.

Monique recognized the look. The mixture of hope and fear. The quiet calculation of what if this doesn't work, that no one ever wanted to admit out loud.

Had it really been fifteen years? Two children, three moves, four promotions, and countless late-night "I'm sorry" conversations since they'd been the ones in those chairs?

Alex squeezed her hand. She turned toward him, and for a moment, time folded in on itself.

It couldn't have been that long. She still saw him the way she had that December 21st—waiting for her at the end of the aisle, smiling and full of love.

He caught her gaze and grinned, that same grin day he changed their first dance song as a surprise.

Alex turned back to the couple and cleared his throat. "So," he said with an easy smile, "you ready to talk about for better or worse?"

Monique laughed softly. "Don't worry," she added. "The worse parts make the better even sweeter."

The young couple relaxed, their shoulders dropping. Outside, the winter light streamed through the church windows.

As Alex started sharing a story about a leaky showerhead and a near-disaster wedding that turned out fine, Monique leaned back in her chair and whispered a quiet prayer of thanks.

For the lessons.

For the laughter.

For love that had grown deeper, stronger, and more faithful with every season.

She couldn't wait to see what the next fifteen years brought.

Book Club Discussion Guide

About the Book:

Monique Lovelace has spent her life dreaming of the perfect Christmas wedding—sparkling lights, soft snow, and her fiancé, Alex Patterson, at the altar. But when the pastors they've chosen to officiate insist they must redo premarital counseling as a nonnegotiable condition, their plans begin to unravel. What follows is a heartfelt—and often hilarious—journey through faith, love, and learning that the path to "I do" isn't always picture-perfect.

With humor, warmth, and a touch of holiday magic, *Christmas Weddings are the ~~Worst~~ Best* reminds readers that love takes patience, honesty, and a willingness to put God at the center of every relationship.

Before You Begin:

Invite readers to reflect on:

- Their favorite holiday memories or wedding stories.
- What "happily ever after" means to them.
- A time when God's timing didn't match their own—but turned out to be perfect.

Encourage them to note quotes, themes, or moments in the book that stood out or made them laugh.

Discussion Questions:

1. First Impressions

- What were your first thoughts about Monique and Alex as a couple?
- Did you find them relatable? Why or why not?
- How did the holiday setting influence your feelings about the story?

2. Faith and Foundations

- How does the requirement to repeat premarital counseling serve as both a conflict and a blessing in disguise?
- What do Monique and Alex learn about faith and commitment through this process?
- Have you ever experienced a situation where God asked you to "start over" with something you thought you'd already mastered?

3. The Perfect vs. The Real

- Monique dreams of a perfect Christmas wedding. What does she learn about perfection versus authenticity?
- How does Alex's perspective balance or challenge Monique's expectations?
- In what ways do societal or social media expectations pressure couples to pursue "perfect" moments?

4. Humor, Honesty, and Healing

- This story balances comedy with real-life relationship challenges. Which scenes made you laugh the most? Which moments made you think deeply?

- How does humor help Monique and Alex face their insecurities?
- Can laughter be an expression of grace?

5. *Lessons in Love*

- What do Monique and Alex's struggles teach about humility, patience, and communication?
- How does their journey mirror real Christian relationships today?
- What message does the book send about letting God lead romantic relationships?

6. *The Role of Community*

- How do friends, family, and pastors contribute to Monique and Alex's growth?
- In what ways do community and mentorship strengthen faith-based marriages?
- How might the church better support couples who are preparing for marriage?

7. *Grace and Growth*

- By the end of the story, how have both Monique and Alex changed?
- What role does forgiveness—of self and each other—play in their healing?
- How does this story illustrate the idea that God's timing is always perfect, even when it feels inconvenient?

8. Christmas Spirit
- How does the Christmas season enhance the emotional impact of the story?
- What symbolic meanings do the holiday traditions carry in the book?
- How does the story remind you of the true meaning of Christmas?

Reflection & Personal Connection:
- How has this story changed or deepened your understanding of love and faith?
- What part of Monique and Alex's journey do you most identify with?
- If you could give Monique and Alex one piece of advice before their wedding day, what would it be?

Creative Activities for Book Clubs:
1. **Share Your "Worst Best" Moment:** Have members share a time when something went hilariously wrong but turned out to be a blessing in disguise.
2. **Letter to Your Future (or Past) Self:** Write a short letter to yourself about trusting God's timing in relationships or life goals.
3. **Christmas Blessing Exchange:** Encourage each member to bring a small token or note representing "grace in imperfection."

4.   **Movie Casting:** Who would you cast as Monique and Alex if this were a Christmas movie?

Scripture Tie-Ins:
- *Ecclesiastes 3:11* — "He has made everything beautiful in its time."
- *1 Corinthians 13:4–7* — The true definition of love.
- *Proverbs 16:9* — "In their hearts humans plan their course, but the Lord establishes their steps."
- *Romans 8:28* — God works all things for good for those who love Him.

For Further Discussion:
- What might happen *after* the story ends?
- How do you imagine Monique and Alex's first Christmas together as a married couple?
- What themes from this book could spark a sequel or companion story in the *Love at Christmas* series?

More From Marie Hobbs:

Unexpected Love Series
Love Next Door (Prequel only available with
newsletter sign-up: www.mariehobbs.com)
Better Than Good
More Than Enough

Love at Christmas Series
Best ~~Worst~~ Christmas Ever
Christmas Weddings are the ~~Worst~~ Best

Stand Alone
Falling for the Grumpy Dad

As a person who fell in love with books before she could read and created stories before she could write, Marie Hobbs is an avid reader. As a hopeful romantic, she read numerous romance novels. As a Christian, she sought out stories with the same values as her own. As she grew older (and hopefully wiser), it became increasingly difficult to find characters she could relate to and books that she could enjoy from cover to cover. She wanted to see herself, her friends, and her family reflected in the books she was reading. Main characters who were people of color thriving in their careers, growing in God, and approaching life with humor and grace. Since she couldn't find enough of the books she wanted to read, she started writing them. Blending real-life experiences, storylines conceived over the years, and creative license, the *Unexpected Love Series* was born—later-in-life inspirational romances with people of color as the main characters.

www.ingramcontent.com/pod-product-compliance
Lightning Source LLC
Chambersburg PA
CBHW072104300726
48975CB00003B/692